Emily Brightwell is the pen name of Cheryl Arguile. She is the author of the Mrs Jeffries murder mystery series, and has also written romance novels as Sarah Temple and Young Adult novels as Cheryl Lanham. She lives in Southern California.

Visit Emily Brightwell's website at
www.emilybrightwell.com

Mrs Jeffries Dusts
for Clues

Emily Brightwell

Published in this paperback edition by C&R Crime,
an imprint of Constable & Robinson Ltd., 2013

Copyright © Cheryl Arguile 1993

A copy of the British Library Cataloguing in
Publication data is available from the British Library

ISBN 978-1-47210-889-0 (paperback)
ISBN 978-1-47210-897-5 (ebook)

Typeset by TW Typesetting, Plymouth, Devon

Printed and bound in the UK

1 3 5 7 9 10 8 6 4 2

CHAPTER ONE

'Most folks is too wrapped up in themselves to pay attention to what's goin' on right under their noses,' Luty Belle Crookshank insisted. 'But I ain't most people. And I know Scotland Yard would still be lookin' for Slocum's murderer if it weren't for you lot. That's why I need your help.'

Mrs Jeffries, the housekeeper for Inspector Gerald Witherspoon of Scotland Yard, wasn't sure she should let Luty's statement pass unchallenged. To be sure, if not for herself and the other servants at Upper Edmonton Gardens, Inspector Witherspoon probably couldn't have solved the Slocum case as quickly as he had, but she had no doubt he would have solved it eventually.

'Now, Luty Belle,' Mrs Jeffries chided. 'That's not precisely true. Inspector Witherspoon had matters well in hand.' She broke off and gestured towards the other servants around the kitchen table. 'We merely helped out a bit.'

' 'Course you did.' Luty gave them a wide, conspiratorial grin. 'I ain't asking you to admit anything, I'm just wantin' a little help.'

Mrs Jeffries glanced at the others. For the first time in three weeks, they didn't look bored. Betsy, the maid, was hanging on Luty Belle's every word. Smythe, the coachman, was grinning from ear to ear. Wiggins, the footman, was leaning forward in his chair so far that Mrs Jeffries was sure if he wasn't careful he'd knock it out from under himself, and Mrs Goodge, the cook, was nodding her head vigorously up and down.

Mrs Jeffries had the distinct impression she'd have a mutiny on her hands if she refused Luty Belle Crook-shank a hearing. Whatever was bothering the elderly American woman, the others wanted to help.

For that matter, so did she. 'All right, Luty Belle. Why don't you tell us what this is all about?'

'Like I said,' Luty began. 'I've got me a problem.'

'What kind of problem?' Betsy asked. She cocked her chin to one side so that one of her blonde curls spilled coquettishly onto her shoulder.

Luty put her teacup on the table. Beneath the fabric of the bright blue-and-lavender-striped dress she wore, her shoulders slumped. 'A real bad one,' she replied slowly, her white head shaking sadly. 'A friend of mine is missing.'

'Someone's missing? Have you reported it to the police?' Mrs Jeffries queried softly.

'Nah, I didn't git worried over the girl until a couple of days ago. Besides, I ain't one to go runnin' to the law about every least little thing. Not that I think that Mary's disappearin' ain't important; it is. But I reckoned you all could do a better job of findin' out what happened to her than the police could. If'n I went to them, they'd just say that Mary's probably run off with some man, and I knows that ain't true.'

'Very wise,' mumbled Mrs Goodge.

'You're right to come ta us,' Smythe added. 'We can find out what happened to yer friend faster than the police.' He flicked a quick glance at Mrs Jeffries. 'No disrespect intended to our inspector,' he explained quickly. 'He's a good copper.'

'Smythe's right,' Betsy interjected. 'You just tell us all about it; we can find her for ya. We're right good at solvin' mysteries.'

'What mystery?' Wiggins asked. He gazed in confusion around the table.

'Haven't you been listenin', boy?' Mrs Goodge admonished. 'Luty's friend 'as disappeared.'

'Oh, sorry.' Wiggins grinned sheepishly. 'I thought she said her friend went visitin'. Guess my mind wandered a bit.'

Luty gave him a sharp look, Smythe and Betsy rolled their eyes, and even Mrs Jeffries had to stifle an impatient sigh. The footman, no doubt, had been daydreaming about his newest infatuation.

'Yes, well perhaps you'd better pay a bit more attention to the conversation, Wiggins,' Mrs Jeffries said firmly. 'And the rest of us had better not make Mrs Crookshank any rash promises. We'd better find out exactly what this is all about before we decide we can resolve the matter.' She turned to Luty Belle. 'Now, who, exactly, is missing?'

'Mary Sparks. She used to be a housemaid at the Lutterbank house. They're my neighbours. They live down at the other end of the gardens. Mary's just a girl, only nineteen, and I'm real worried about her.'

'We can see that.' Mrs Jeffries nodded. 'How long has she been gone?'

Luty sighed. 'Two months.'

'And you're just now startin' to look fer her?' Smythe asked in disbelief. 'Cor, anythin' could have 'appened to 'er by now.'

'That's a long time for a body to be lost,' Wiggins added thoughtfully.

'If it's been two months,' Betsy put in sombrely, 'she in't missing, she's dead.'

'For goodness' sake,' Mrs Jeffries exclaimed as she saw the elderly woman turn pale, 'will you all please stop scaring Luty? We can't make any assumptions about what has or has not happened to Mary Sparks until we hear the rest of the story.'

Luty Belle smiled gratefully and took a deep breath. 'I reckon I'd better start at the beginning. About two months ago, I was fixin' to go to Venice. As it turned out, I shouldn'a bothered. Smelly place. Waste of money, but that's neither here nor there. But you need to know what took me so long to start frettin' over the girl.' She paused. 'Anyhows, a few days before I was leavin', Mary come over and she was cryin' and carryin' on like she'd just lost her best friend. When I got her calmed down, she told me the Lutterbanks had let her go. Seems they accused her of stealing a silver brooch.'

'Had she stolen the brooch?' Mrs Jeffries asked quickly.

Luty shook her head. 'Nah. The girl's no thief. I know that for a fact.'

Smythe raised an eyebrow. 'What makes ya so sure?'

''Cause that's how me and Mary became friends,' Luty replied tartly. 'I got acquainted with the girl when she returned my fur muff. I'd dropped it in the gardens, and furthermore, young man, that muff was stuffed with money. Now if'n Mary Sparks was a thief, she wouldn't have bothered to give the danged thing back to me, would she?'

'Nah, if'n she were a thief, she'd 'ave kept it,' he agreed.

'What happened then?' Betsy said hastily.

'I told Mary she could stay at my place until I got back and then we'd sort everything out. But Mary wasn't one for acceptin' charity. All she wanted me to do was to write her a letter of reference to one of them domestic employment agencies. She'd heard about a position with some preacher's family over in Putney. So that's what I did.' Luty grasped her hands together. 'The next day, the agency give her the job. She come back to my place, picked up her carpetbag and said goodbye. I went on to Venice. It wasn't until a few days ago, when I realized that I hadn't received any letters from her, that I got worried.'

'Mary could read and write?' Betsy asked.

'Yup, that's one of the reasons we became friends. Mary and I both liked to read. I used to loan her some of my books.' The harsh set of Luty's jaw softened as she smiled. Then the moment passed and she continued. 'But that's neither here nor there. As I was sayin', I started to fret over not hearin' from Mary, so I sent my butler to the Everdene house, that's the place where Mary was goin' to work, to check on the girl.

But when Hatchet got back, he told me the Everdenes claim Mary up and quit the day after she arrived.'

'Could she have gone back to her family?' Mrs Goodge asked. She pushed another plate of buns towards Luty Belle.

'Nah. Mary didn't have no family. She'd been on her own since she was fourteen.' Luty Belle picked up a currant bun and put it on her plate. Mrs Jeffries nodded thoughtfully. 'Did the Everdenes say where she'd gone?'

'Hatchet didn't think to ask,' Luty replied in disgust. 'I was thinkin' of going there myself and seein' what I could find out.'

'I think you'd better let one o' us do that,' Smythe said quickly.

'Why?' Luty's black eyes narrowed dangerously. 'You think I couldn't get that toffee-nosed bunch to answer my questions?'

'Of course you could,' Mrs Jeffries said soothingly. 'But I'm afraid I must agree with Smythe. You should leave the task to us. If they've lied to your butler, they'll probably lie to you as well. We've got better ways of finding out the truth.'

'Yeah, I reckon you're right at that. There's no tellin' what kind of tales that preacher might make up.' Luty snorted. 'Never did much trust preachers.'

'Have you asked the Lutterbanks if they've heard from her?' Mrs Jeffries asked.

'Nah,' Luty said grimly. 'I knows that bunch too well to bother talkin' to them. Old Mrs Lutterbank is as crazy as a bedbug, Mr Lutterbank is a pompous windbag, Fiona wouldn't know the truth if'n it walked up and pinched her on the cheek, and Andrew is such a slippery varmint, I wouldn't trust him to tell me the sun rose in the east and set in the west.'

'Gracious, you certainly don't sound as though you care for them overly much.' Mrs Jeffries cocked her head to one side. 'Do you think they may have had something to do with Mary's disappearance?'

'I'm not sure. But I've seen the likes of Andrew Lutterbank before. He's a mean, vicious bastard, and I know he had a right yen for Mary. But she weren't havin' none of that. Mary's a good girl, and she was too smart to risk her employment by prettyin' up to a no-count varmint like him.' Luty shrugged. 'But much as I dislike that bunch, I don't think they had anythin' to do with Mary bein' missin'. From what I've heard, Andrew's walkin' a fine line these days. The last time he got a housemaid in trouble, it cost him five hundred pounds and a trip to Australia. Nah, he might have had his eye on Mary, but I reckon he left her alone.'

Betsy gazed at Luty Belle sympathetically. 'Did Mary have any other friends? Did she go out on her day off with any of the other housemaids?'

'Well,' Luty Belle replied thoughtfully, 'she was friendly with Garrett, the groundskeeper's assistant. But he's three years younger than her, and she's practically engaged to his older brother, Mark. But Mark's away at sea, so I knows she didn't go to him. Sometimes, I'd see her walkin' about in the gardens with Cassie Yates.'

'Where could we find this Cassie Yates?' Smythe asked. He leaned forward on his elbows and clasped his big hands together under his chin.

'Cassie's a shop assistant at MacLeod's. They're on the King's Road. I reckon you can find her there.' Luty Belle shook her head. 'Other than those two and myself, Mary kept pretty much to herself. She's a quiet little thing.' She fixed her gaze on the far wall, and her lower lip started to tremble. 'I'm so scared somethin' awful's happened to Mary.' Luty blinked furiously and got ahold of herself when she realized they were all staring at her sympathetically.

'Perhaps,' Mrs Jeffries suggested gently, 'she's found a . . . well, sweetheart, and eloped?'

'She'd have let me know,' Luty Belle insisted. 'Don't you git it? Mary and me was friends. She promised to write, to keep in touch. But I ain't heard a peep from her. And even if'n she decided she didn't love Mark McGraw and had gone off with some smooth-talkin' man, she'd have written me.'

Betsy reached over and touched the old lady's arm. 'Mrs Crookshank.'

'I told ya to call me Luty Belle.'

'Sorry, Luty Belle, Mary may have gone off with someone and, well, been ashamed to let you know about it. Especially, if'n he didn't marry 'er. It 'appens, you know.'

Mrs Goodge nodded wisely and Wiggins blushed.

'Nah. Mary wouldn't have been ashamed. Not with me.'

'On the day that Mary came to you, did you give her any money?' Mrs Jeffries asked briskly.

'I tried to, but she wouldn't take a penny. All she wanted was one night's lodgin' and a letter of reference.' Luty Belle suddenly stood up. 'Are you goin' to help me

8

or not?' she demanded. ' 'Causin' if you ain't, I reckon I'll have to start lookin' myself or hire me one of them private inquiry agents. But come hell or high water, I'm goin' to find out what happened to Mary Sparks.'

Mrs Jeffries gazed around the table. Each time her eyes met one of the others', there was a barely perceptible nod to show accord. They all wanted her to say yes.

'Of course we're going to help you,' Mrs Jeffries stated calmly.

'I ain't askin' any of you to do it fer free,' Luty Belle announced. When they all started to protest, she held up her hand. 'Quit your caterwaulin'. I ain't goin' to insult anyone by offering you money. Agreed?'

Betsy's eyebrows lifted, Smythe looked amused, Mrs Goodge pursed her lips, and Wiggins grinned happily. Mrs Jeffries cleared her throat. They all turned and stared at her expectantly, waiting for her to speak for them. Mrs Jeffries wasn't quite sure what to say. She opened her mouth and then closed it. She could hardly refuse Luty's offer. If she did, she was sure the American woman wouldn't let them help. Luty Belle was too proud for that. And she knew that if the household lost this chance to do a bit of detective work, they'd all be utterly miserable.

'Um, Luty,' she began, trying to think of a delicate way to tell her payment of any kind would be rather uncomfortable.

'You look like a gaping fish, Hepzibah.' Luty put her hands on her hips. 'Now, I knows you're all proud as pikestaffs, and I told you I ain't offerin' you money. Let's just say that no matter what you find out, I'll do what's right and we'll leave it at that.

Mrs Jeffries smiled. 'That will be just fine, Luty.'

They got a few more details about Mary Sparks out of Luty Belle, and then she left. As soon as the kitchen door had closed behind her, they all started talking at once.

'The girl's probably run off with some man,' Mrs Goodge said darkly as she began to gather up the tea things.

'Or she could have been sold into white slavery,' Betsy said.

'If the girl's been missin' for two months,' Smythe added, 'she's probably at the bottom of the Thames.'

'Maybe she's gone to America,' Wiggins said cheerfully.

'Really,' Mrs Jeffries said. 'You all have most appalling ideas. I'm glad you managed to keep some of those rather depressing opinions to yourself. Poor Luty Belle's worried enough.'

'What do you think 'appened to her, then?' Betsy stuffed the last bite of currant bun into her mouth and then nimbly got to her feet and took the plate to the sink.

'That's impossible to say right now,' Mrs Jeffries replied. 'But we'll do our best to find out. Wiggins, I want you to get over to Knightsbridge and talk to Garrett McGraw.'

Wiggins's round face creased in worry as he pursed his lips. 'What should I ask?'

'Find out everything you can about Mary Sparks and about the Lutterbank family.' Mrs Jeffries turned to Betsy. 'Would you like to go shopping?'

'Want me to question Cassie Yates, do ya?' Betsy

grinned from ear to ear, her blue eyes sparkling with the thrill of the hunt. 'I'll find out anythin' I can.'

Smythe cleared his throat and crossed his arms over his massive chest. His big brutal face was set in an expression of feigned boredom, but his dark brown eyes were sparkling as brightly as Betsy's. 'I suppose you want me to go back to them miserable pubs in Knightsbridge.'

'If you wouldn't mind,' Mrs Jeffries replied sweetly. She knew Smythe was teasing her a little. He'd got an enormous amount of information on the murder of Dr Slocum from hanging about those Knightsbridge pubs. For all his complaints, Mrs Jeffries knew he enjoyed his forays.

She turned to Mrs Goodge. The cook gazed back at her knowingly. 'I expect I can remember a bit of gossip about the Lutterbanks,' she said calmly. 'But you'd better give me a few hours. The name hasn't rung any bells yet.'

Mrs Jeffries nodded. Mrs Goodge knew every morsel of gossip about every important family in London. Like Smythe, she too had come up with some invaluable bits and pieces during the Slocum investigation.

'Are we goin' to mention the girl to the inspector?' Betsy asked as she pulled on her gloves.

'Not right away,' Mrs Jeffries replied. 'We may have to eventually, but for right now, we'll see what we can come up with on our own. We don't want to bother him unless it becomes absolutely necessary.'

The inspector was kept completely in the dark about their activities. None of them wanted the dear man to think they lacked confidence in his skills as a dectective. 'But I will ask him some discreet questions when he gets home,' she continued. 'He should be able to tell us if any young female bodies have turned up in the last two months.'

Betsy made a face. She was turning into an excellent detective, but she was really quite squeamish.

Mrs Jeffries waited until everyone had left and then she sighed in satisfaction. There was nothing like a mystery to lift one's spirits.

Magpie Lane had been almost obliterated. Where there had once been a row of tiny redbrick houses, there were now only piles of rubble and debris. The one house that hadn't been torn down stood alone at the end of the street, a forlorn shell with no windows and the doors haphazardly boarded over. On the other side of the road was an abandoned brewery enclosed by a twelve-foot wall.

Inspector Gerald Witherspoon slowed his steps as he followed Constable Barnes to the far end of the street. Three workmen and two uniformed police constables were standing over an open trench. 'She's in there, sir,' the taller of two constables called. He pointed down into what had once been the cellar of a house. 'We sent for CID as soon as we realized the remains were human, sir.'

'Thank you, Constable.' Witherspoon gulped and studiously avoided looking down. 'Constable Barnes,' he ordered, 'you'd best see to it.'

Barnes hurried down the ladder someone had stuck at the side. A moment later, Witherspoon's worst fears were confirmed.

'It's a body, all right, Inspector,' Barnes called cheerfully. 'You'd best come down and see for yourself.'

There was no hope for it, he had to look at the corpse. Witherspoon didn't like dead bodies. Despite his being a police officer, his stomach was really quite delicate. As he descended the ladder, he found himself hoping that this body would be as tidy as his last one, but considering it had been in the ground, he thought that was rather a faint hope. He was right.

He stopped at the bottom of the ladder, took a deep breath and then walked over to stand next to Barnes. Keeping his gaze level with the top of the trench, he silently prayed he wouldn't be sick or, even worse, that he wouldn't disgrace himself by fainting. He took another deep breath and then immediately wished he hadn't. Now that the remains had been exposed, the smell was awful. The air in the confined space was filled with the sickeningly sweet stench of decaying flesh.

Witherspoon's stomach turned over.

'Looks like it's a woman,' Barnes said. He stepped back to give his inspector room. Witherspoon was trapped now. He had to look.

The corpse was lying on its side, the face turned into the flat dirt of the trench. He could see that she was wearing a dark blue dress and that her hair, which had once been blonde, was tangled with matted earth.

'Yes,' the inspector mumbled, 'so it appears.' He knelt down and held his breath.

'Shouldn't we turn 'er over?' Barnes asked.

Witherspoon shuddered as he forced his hands to touch the dead shoulders. Keeping his head down so

13

no one would see that his eyes were closed, he pulled the body onto its back.

Barnes made a funny choking noise. 'Cor, this one's bad.'

A wave of nausea washed through the inspector, but he grimly reminded himself of his duty. 'Get out your notebook, Constable,' Witherspoon ordered. Perhaps, he thought, it would be best to get this over with as quickly as possible.

'Right, sir.'

'Uhmm, well. The body is that of a woman.' He forced himself to open his eyes and then almost gagged. 'The face is black and bloated. Virtually unrecognizable.'

'Blimey, don't you want to put a handkerchief over your nose?' Barnes asked the inspector. 'She's gettin' riper by the minute.'

'No, no, I'm quite all right,' Witherspoon lied. He knew if he didn't get this done quickly, he'd never be able to force himself back into this hole. 'The deceased is wearing a heavy . . .' he broke off and tentatively touched the material of the dress, '. . . wool dress. It's a dark blue.'

'Any sign of what killed her, sir?' Barnes glanced down at the body, and his lips curled in disgust. 'Cor, that's obvious, isn't it? Looks like there's a great big gapin' hole in her chest. Think she's been stabbed, sir?'

'Yes, Constable,' the inspector replied faintly, 'it certainly seems so.' He quickly averted his gaze from the wound. 'We must be sure and have our lads do more digging to see if the weapon is here as well.'

'What kind of knife do you think it was, sir?' the Constable asked cheerfully.

'I really shouldn't like to say at this point in the investigation.'

'Right, sir. She got a weddin' ring on?'

Witherspoon glanced at what was left of her hands, then quickly looked away. 'Difficult to tell, Constable. But we must make sure we instruct the searchers to look for one. It could have slipped off when the flesh was . . .' He broke off, wondering just how to phrase the truly horrendous thought. When the flesh was eaten by rats or decomposed or whatever wretched force of nature had caused the poor girl's hands to be nothing but bones.

'She must have had money,' Barnes said. 'Look, that brooch on her dress looks like silver.'

Witherspoon hadn't even noticed the jewellery. He glanced at the horseshoe-shaped silver pin, saw that it was so encrusted with dirt and mud that it was impossible to identify the small stones set along the top of the curve, and then looked away. 'Not necessarily, Constable. Someone may have given it to her. For all we know, the poor woman may have been as poor as a church mouse. It's a bit too early to start making assumptions.'

Barnes knelt down and pointed at the feet. 'You're probably right, sir,' he said. 'But them shoes look like good quality.' He leaned to one side, stared at the corpse's foot and then reached over and began brushing the dirt away from the sole. 'Inspector, these shoes are new.'

'Really?' Witherspoon answered curiously. 'How can you tell?'

The constable continued his assault on the shoes.

'Because this dirt here is from being buried, but when you brush it away, these soles look like new. See, look 'ere, there isn't even a scuff mark.'

'Yes,' Witherspoon replied weakly, after one fast look at the shoes, 'I see what you mean. Good observation, Constable.' Actually, he didn't have any idea whether it was a good observation or not, but he felt he must say something.

'Cor, she's got right big feet for someone her size, hasn't she?'

'Someone her size,' Witherspoon mumbled. Oh dear, if he didn't get out of this pit, he really would faint.

'Sure, she's a little thing. Doesn't look more than a bit over five foot.'

Abruptly, Witherspoon stood up and headed for the ladder. 'See to the body, Constable,' he called as he climbed out into the blessed fresh air. 'I'm going to talk to the man who found her.'

Witherspoon took a few moments to catch his breath before advancing on the three workmen who stood a few feet away, their shovels and picks sticking straight up out of the soft ground.

'Which of you gentlemen found the er . . . body?' he asked.

'It were me,' the largest of the three said. He took off his cap and stepped forward. 'I be the leadman. Jack Cawley.'

'Er . . . yes. Could you tell me precisely how you happened upon the er . . . deceased.'

'Well, I were diggin', weren't I. Mind you, I wouldn't have been diggin' if them fools hadn't flooded out that trench over on Ormond Street. We'd a never been here if them stupid engineers knew what they was doing.' Cawley snorted in disgust.

'Inspector,' Barnes called excitedly as he came out of the pit. 'I found this around her neck. It's a necklace of some kind.' He held the dirt-encrusted object out to the inspector. 'And it's got a ring on it. Maybe she was married after all.'

Wrinkling his nose, Witherspoon took the necklace and examined the ring. 'A married woman wouldn't wear her wedding ring around her neck,' he said. He flaked a bit more dirt off the ring and held it up to the light. 'I don't think this is a wedding ring.'

Through the layers of grime, he could see the dull yellow glint of gold. Scraping more dirt off, he saw three dark blue stones set between filigreed patterns on the metal. The ring was valuable. He suspected the stones might be sapphires. Drat, whoever had murdered the girl hadn't robbed her. Witherspoon sighed deeply. A dead girl and an expensive ring usually meant trouble. Complications. A nasty case. Perhaps even a crime of passion.

'Could it be a betrothal ring?' Barnes asked.

'A what?'

'A betrothal ring. Engaged couples wear 'em. Though I don't know why. Seems to me a good plain weddin' band should be enough for most folks. But that don't seem to be good enough for young people these days,' the constable said as he shook his head.

'Yes, I suppose it could be.' Witherspoon turned back to the workman he'd been talking with. 'Now, as you were saying.'

17

'I were saying if it hadn't been for them fool engineers, we'd never have found 'er.'

'I'm sorry,' Witherspoon said. 'I don't really follow you. What do the engineers have to do with your finding the body?'

Cawley's bushy eyebrows rose. 'It's got everythin' to do with it. We wouldn't have been diggin' up Magpie Lane if they hadn't flooded the other trench.' He pointed towards the body. 'We wouldn't have been here fer another six months if they hadn't flooded out Ormond Street. With all the damp and the vermin down where she's been layin', she'd've been dust by the time we'd got here – if we'd stuck to our schedule. Probably wouldn't have even been the shoes left.'

'Exactly what are you digging?' Witherspoon asked. He wasn't sure that was a particularly pertinent question, but he felt he should ask.

'A new Underground line. The Underground were supposed to be under Ormond Street and a new road here on Magpie Lane. But them fools made a mistake 'cause Ormond Street sits on a bleedin' buried stream.' Cawley shook his head. 'So at the last minute, they change their bloomin' minds and send us over here to start hacking up Magpie Lane. This here's the first trench – this time, they decided they wanted to make sure there weren't no water before they brought in the heavy diggers.'

'I see.' Witherspoon nodded. 'And you're the one that actually found the er . . . remains?'

Cawley grunted. 'Not very pretty either. 'Ere I was, diggin' away and me shovel all of a sudden hits her foot. Well, I weren't sure what it was when I first hit it, so me and the blokes just kept on going diggin'. You can see what we found. As soon as we realized it were a body, we sent for the coppers.'

'Inspector,' Barnes called again. 'How deep should I have the lads dig? Whoever killed her may have buried the weapon under the body.'

Witherspoon had no idea. He took a wild guess. 'Oh, have them go down another foot or so. And be sure to do a house-to-house as soon as you're finished searching the trench.'

'House-to-house?' Barnes asked in confusion.

Witherspoon remembered there weren't any houses. 'I meant, a house-to-house up on the main road.'

'And what will they be asking, sir?'

'On second thoughts, Constable, I think we'd better delay that part of the investigation until after we've identified the victim.' He hurriedly turned back to Cawley. 'You don't, by any chance, happen to know when the houses on this street were demolished, do you?'

' 'Fraid not,' the workman replied. 'I don't live around these parts. But Fred might know. He lives 'round 'ere.' Turning, he called to one of the two workmen standing a few yards away. 'Get over here, Fred. The copper wants to ask you some questions.'

The small, wiry man didn't look pleased, but he pushed away from the shovel he was leaning on and walked towards the inspector.

'What is your name?' the inspector asked.

'Fred Tompkins.'

'And I understand you live nearby. Could you please tell me when these houses were torn down?'

'About a month ago,' he replied sullenly. 'Everyone who lived here was evicted, thrown out on the streets just so they could tear down some perfectly good 'omes. It were a crime, that's what it was. A crime. Throwing people out of their 'omes just so some toff could tear 'em down and sell the land to build a bloody road.'

Witherspoon watched the man sympathetically. 'I take it the locals weren't too pleased,' he said softly.

'We hated it. Me own sister lost her 'ome.' He turned and pointed towards the one remaining house. 'She used to live right next to that one. Nice little place it was. Good solid redbrick, plenty of space in the back for her vegetable plot, and she gets tossed out, without so much as a by-your-leave. They only give her a few days to pack up her belongings. She had to move to a grotty set of rooms in Lambeth. And her with three kids and a sick 'usband.'

'I'm sorry,' Witherspoon said sincerely. 'So the residents were suddenly told they had to leave. Do you happen to know who owns these properties?'

Tompkins's lips curled in disgust. 'Weren't no owners, leastways, not like real landlords. This whole street was owned by a property company, so there weren't even someone to complain to.' He kicked at a loose stone and sent it flying. 'Hard-hearted bastards.'

'Do you know the name of the company?' Witherspoon wished the police surgeon would get there. The smell of the corpse was getting stronger.

'No. But I can ask my sister. She got a letter from 'em and the name were written right at the top.'

'Thank you. That would be most helpful.' He pulled

out his notebook and took down the man's address. 'I'll send a constable around tomorrow for the information.'

There was a tap on Witherspoon's shoulder. Startled, he whirled around and found himself staring into the familiar face of Inspector Nigel Nivens.

'Goodness, Inspector Nivens, you gave me such a shock. What are you doing down here?'

Nigel Nivens was a sharp-nosed, pale-faced man with cool grey eyes, slicked-back dark blond hair and a thin mouth. He gave Witherspoon a weak smile. 'I thought I'd come down and see if you needed any assistance. I understand you've been given another murder.'

'I'd hardly put it in those terms, Inspector,' Witherspoon said lightly, 'I really don't feel like I've been given anything.' Then he silently chided himself. Inspector Nivens's turn of phrase was no doubt unintentional. Perhaps he was even being sympathetic. But dear, he did make it sound so odd. Witherspoon knew he was being given another wretched murder to solve; not a nice present for Christmas.

Inspector Nivens looked towards the open trench. 'Is it in there?'

'Yes, I'm afraid so. It's a woman.'

'Definitely murdered?'

'Yes. She's been stabbed.' Witherspoon sighed. 'It's jolly kind of you to offer your assistance, but I'm afraid I can't allow you to help. You know how the Chief Inspector feels, one senior officer to a case. Gracious, if two inspectors are tied up on one case, he'd be most annoyed.'

'Humph, I suppose you're right.' Nivens looked longingly towards the trench. 'But it doesn't really seem fair.

After all, this is your second murder in a row. I should think, Witherspoon, that it would be only sporting to give someone else a chance.' He mumbled something under his breath. Inspector Witherspoon couldn't quite make out what he said, but he did hear the word 'competent'.

'It really isn't my decision, now, is it?' Witherspoon said soothingly. 'Perhaps if you had a word with the Chief Inspector . . .'

'Wouldn't do any good. For some reason, he thinks you're a genius when it comes to murder.' Nivens smiled coolly. 'It'll be interesting to see how you do with this one. Perhaps it won't be as simple as the Slocum murder.'

Witherspoon was slightly offended. Finding the murderer of Dr Bartholomew Slocum had been anything but simple. And he didn't really understand what Inspector Nivens was complaining about. The fellow always got good, clean burglaries. Lucky man.

CHAPTER TWO

MRS JEFFRIES WAS waiting in the hallway when Inspector Witherspoon arrived home. 'Good evening, sir,' she said cheerfully as she took his bowler hat and coat. 'Have you had a good day?'

She knew he hadn't had a particularly good day. One look at his long face had told her that much. But she wasn't deterred, certain a cosy chat and a nice glass of sherry would no doubt fix him right up.

'Good evening, Mrs Jeffries,' Witherspoon replied. 'As a matter of fact, it's been a very dreadful sort of day.'

'Oh dear, I'm so sorry to hear that.' She turned towards the drawing room. 'But not to worry, you'll feel much better after you've had a chance to relax.'

The inspector dutifully followed her into the drawing room and sat down in his favourite wing chair. A fire blazed in the hearth, a glass of amber liquid was sitting on the table next to his chair, and Mrs Jeffries was gazing at him sympathetically. He felt much better already.

'What delight is Mrs Goodge cooking up for our dinner tonight?' he asked as he reached for his glass.

Mrs Jeffries desperately wanted to know whether the inspector knew of any unidentifed female bodies turning up in the last two months. But she didn't want to arouse her employer's curiosity. Not just yet. There would be time enough for that after she and the others had done more investigating into Mary's disappearance. She curbed her impatience and decided to wait until he had some sherry in him before she brought up the subject. Besides, the inspector was always far more willing to talk on a full stomach.

'Roast pork and poached apples,' she replied with a smile. 'Now, Inspector, tell me all about it.'

'About what?'

'Why, your dreadful day, of course.' She gazed at him earnestly. 'I know you never like to complain, but really, sir, sometimes it helps to get things off one's chest. As soon as you walked into the house this evening, I knew something utterly appalling must have happened.'

'You're so very perceptive, Mrs Jeffries,' he murmured with a relieved sigh. 'And you're absolutely right, as usual. There's been a murder. A very difficult one, I'm afraid.'

'How terrible.' Mrs Jeffries tried to sound appropriately subdued, but it was difficult. Not that she condoned murder, naturally. Yet she couldn't help but be elated by the fact that she and the rest of the household would now have two cases to work on. Not only would they find the missing Mary Sparks, but they could help their dear inspector as well. 'Why do you think this one's going to be difficult?'

'Because the body was only found today.'

Witherspoon paused and took a deep breath. 'And the murder was committed several months ago.'

'Several months ago!' Mrs Jeffries was scandalized. The trail would be colder than a February frost.

'Perhaps even more. The police surgeon was only guessing when he made that estimate.' The inspector drained the rest of his drink. 'I tell you, Mrs Jeffries, the world has become an evil place. Imagine, this poor girl dead, stabbed right through the heart and buried in the bottom of some cellar and no one even notices she's missing. You'd think that when a person didn't appear as usual, someone would take the time and trouble to notify the police.'

Mrs Jeffries refused to jump to a conclusion. Just because Inspector Witherspoon had found the body of a woman didn't mean that the body was Mary Sparks. Despite what the good inspector said, she knew dozens of people disappeared all the time in the city and no one bothered to tell the police. 'That's appalling. I take it the deceased is a young woman?'

'Yes. Dreadful, isn't it.'

'How old was the victim?'

'We're not absolutely sure. The best the police surgeon could do is give us an estimate. He thinks she couldn't have been more than twenty-five, but naturally, we'll know more after the post-mortem.'

Mrs Jeffries asked, 'Do you know who she is?'

'No, I'm afraid not.' Remembering the state of the body, he shuddered. 'Unfortunately, she'd been in the ground so long her face is unrecognizable. But she was smallish, only an inch or so over five feet tall and she had blonde hair.'

Mrs Jeffries didn't like the sound of that. 'Oh dear, however are you going to find out who the poor girl was?' She reminded herself that there were hundreds of women who had blonde hair.

'We're comparing her description to those we have of missing women. Hopefully, we'll turn up something soon. It'll be very hard to find out who murdered her if we don't know who she is, er, was.' He shook his head. 'But we don't really have much to go on.'

'Not to worry, Inspector,' Mrs Jeffries said briskly. 'I'm sure you'll find out everything you need to know and solve this case just as you've solved all the others. Was there anything unusual about the way she was dressed? Anything that would give you a clue?'

'Not really. She was wearing a good-quality blue dress and she had several pieces of jewellery on her person. But it's the sort of dress one sees everywhere. You know, very much like the one that Betsy wears on her day out.' He shrugged. 'I don't see that her clothing will be of much use, more's the pity.'

'Perhaps you'll have better luck with the jewellery. What kind was it?' Mrs Jeffries asked cautiously. 'A wedding ring, perhaps.'

She sincerely hoped it was. If the victim had been married, it almost definitely wasn't Mary Sparks who had been found. But Mrs Jeffries's hopes were quickly dashed.

'Oh no,' the inspector said. 'Not quite. I believe the object we found is more properly called a "betrothal ring",' Witherspoon explained. 'But the odd thing was she didn't have the ring on her finger, as one would expect. She wore it round her neck on a small gold chain. There was a silver brooch on the lapel of her dress as well. Both pieces looked quite valuable.'

'That should help you determine her identity,' Mrs Jeffries replied slowly. Her mind was working frantically. She wished she'd asked Luty Belle if the brooch Mary Sparks had been accused of stealing had ever turned up at the Lutterbank house. She made a mental note to talk to Luty tomorrow morning.

'I certainly hope so. I mean the girl was well dressed and had expensive jewellery on her person. She must be someone important. You'd think someone, somewhere would have reported her missing.'

'One would think so,' Mrs Jeffries agreed. 'Obviously the murder wasn't committed as part of a robbery.'

'Uhmm, that was a bit of hard luck. After all, a robber would hardly have left a valuable ring and brooch on his victim.' Witherspoon sighed dramatically. 'A simple robbery would have been most helpful. It would certainly make this case easier to solve.'

Mrs Jeffries stared at him curiously. 'Do you really think so?'

'But of course.' Witherspoon put his glass down. 'Thieves have to sell their ill-gotten gains somewhere,' he explained, 'and we've got quite good connections into the criminal classes these days. Why, Inspector Nivens has several sources of information he regularly taps when it comes to robberies. Now if we'd been lucky on this case, the poor girl would have been robbed before she was murdered. I could then have quite legitimately taken Inspector Nivens up on his kind offer of assistance.'

'Inspector Nivens offered to help you with this case?' Mrs Jeffries asked carefully, striving to remain calm.

'Oh, yes,' Witherspoon answered as he glanced at the clock on the mantelpiece. 'He came round Magpie Lane today as soon as he'd heard a body was discovered. Most thoughtful of him. But naturally, I couldn't accept. You know the Chief Inspector's views on having more than one senior officer on a case.'

By sheer willpower, Mrs Jeffries managed to restrain herself from blurting out precisely what she thought of Inspector Nigel Nivens. Her dear inspector was far too innocent about some things. But it was obvious to her that Nigel Nivens was just waiting for his chance to ruin Gerald Witherspoon. Why, the man had once had the audacity to complain to the Chief Inspector that Inspector Witherspoon must be getting outside help on the cases he'd solved. If Nivens was going to be snooping around on this murder, and she had no doubt that he was, they'd have to be very careful. Very careful indeed.

'Do you think Mrs Goodge has dinner ready yet?' Witherspoon asked.

Mrs Jeffries deliberately kept the conversation away from bodies and murder as she ushered the inspector into the dining room. She waited until he was well tucked into his supper before mentioning the subject again.

Witherspoon, who really wanted to get the horrid experience off his chest, soon told her every little detail about finding the body and questioning the workman. He particularly enjoyed repeating Jack Cawley's remarks about the stupidity of engineers and local officials.

'And really, Mrs Jeffries,' he continued as he helped himself to another serving of poached apples, managing to edge a slice of apple onto the rim of the plate, 'I'm amazed at how callous some people are.'

Mrs Jeffries snatched a spoon and shoved the apple back into the dish before it landed on the white linen tablecloth. 'People aren't really callous, sir,' she said soothingly. 'I expect they merely say whatever pops into their heads as a way of dealing with the horror of it. Finding a body when one is digging a trench must come as a bit of a shock.'

The inspector raised his eyebrows. 'I wasn't referring to the workman who found the body, I was referring to Constable Barnes. No doubt, there's much truth to what you say, but really, I thought it most ungallant of the man to mention what big feet the victim had.' He paused, remembering what else Barnes had said. 'But then again, if he hadn't commented on her feet, we might not have noticed she was wearing new shoes.'

'New shoes?' Mrs Jeffries cocked her chin to one side. 'But if the body had been in the ground for two months, how could you tell? Weren't the feet encrusted with dirt?'

'Scuff marks.' He smiled triumphantly. 'There weren't any scuff marks on the soles. Once the dirt was brushed away, it was very obvious the lady had put on a pair of brand-new shoes. Good leather too, good quality.'

'I suppose you've already got the constable out looking for the shop that sold them.'

Witherspoon frowned. 'Do you think that's necessary? We're hoping to identify the victim by tracking down the jewellery. Both the brooch and the ring are somewhat unusual. It should be easy enough to find the shop that sold them.'

'But what if the victim didn't purchase either of them? Perhaps they were gifts. Women don't often buy jewellery for themselves.'

'Oh, that doesn't matter,' Witherspoon replied airily. 'I've already thought of that possibility. A girl hardly buys her own betrothal ring. Once we find where the jewellery was purchased, it'll be quite easy to obtain the name of the person who bought the items. When we know that name, we'll soon know the name of our victim. I suspect the betrothal ring, at least, was bought by a man for his young lady. He's bound to know who she is, er, was.'

'I take it you're assuming that whoever bought it was engaged to the victim?'

'Well, that had crossed my mind.'

'Then why hasn't he reported her missing?' Mrs Jeffries asked blandly.

'Er, perhaps he doesn't know she's gone,' Witherspoon mumbled. But even to his own ears, that sounded like nonsense. Drat! Why hadn't the man reported his fiancée missing? If, indeed, she was someone's fiancée. But perhaps she wasn't. Perhaps she was something else, something else entirely.

Witherspoon's face fell as he realized just how many problems he might be facing. Perhaps he would have Constable Barnes try to trace the shoes as well. 'You know, I do believe I will have Barnes see if he can find out who sold our victim her shoes. Can't afford to ignore any line of inquiry, can I?'

'Why, you've never done that, sir,' Mrs Jeffries said hastily as she saw his gloomy expression. 'You're a most efficient policeman. You never leave any stone unturned. Why you've foiled the most diabolically clever murderers, and I'm sure you'll do the same for this last unfortunate victim.'

Her words cheered him instantly. 'Oh, please, Mrs Jeffries.' Witherspoon flushed with pleasure at her praise. 'You're being far too kind. I'm merely a simple man. I do my duty to God, Queen and Country and hope that my small, insignificant contribution makes the world a better place.'

The sun was shining brightly as Mrs Jeffries came into the kitchen the next morning. Betsy, Smythe, Wiggins and Mrs Goodge were already sitting around the table, waiting for her.

'Good morning, everyone,' she said as she took her seat. 'I trust that everyone was successful yesterday?'

'Absolutely, Mrs J.' Smythe grinned. 'As a matter of fact, you'd best let me talk first today. I thinks you'll be right interested in what I've come across.'

' 'Ow come you get ta go first?' Betsy asked.

' 'Cause as soon as Mrs J hears what I've found out, I expect she'll be wantin' me to go out agin.'

Betsy started to protest, thought better of it, and contented herself with a sniff.

'Please proceed, Smythe,' Mrs Jeffries said quickly.

'Well, it's all right mysterious. One of the Lutter-banks' footman told me he saw Mary Sparks back in the communal gardens on the evenin' of September the tenth. That's two days after she quit workin' for 'em.'

'Two days? Are you sure?' Mrs Jeffries frowned. 'Luty Belle said Mary only stayed the one night. What would she have been doing back in Knightsbridge the following evening? She was supposed to have been working for the Everdenes by then.'

Smythe nodded. 'I'm sure. The footman was definite about the dates. He remembers because the tenth was always the day that Andrew Lutterbank got his quarterly allowance from his father. But on September the tenth, the old man refused to give it out. Instead, he and Andrew had a right old shoutin' match. Every servant in the bloomin' 'ouse 'eard the two of 'em goin' at it. Wesley, that's the footman, finally couldn't stand it any more so he took himself out to the garden to get away from the screamin'. While he was out there, he saw Mary Sparks.'

'What time was this?' Mrs Jeffries asked.

'He weren't sure, but he said it had just gone dark when he seen her. Spotted her hangin' about at the gate near the far end. He's a right nosey 'un. Wondered what she were doin', her havin' left and all.'

'How long did she hang about by the gate?' Mrs Goodge asked curiously.

Smythe grinned. 'Long enough to watch Andrew Lutterbank leavin' in a huff. Wesley thought that was right peculiar too, said Mary were just hoverin' down the far end when all of a sudden his nibs trots out the back door and flies down the path like the 'ounds of 'ades was on his 'eels. Well, Mary looked right surprised, and she jumped into that tangle of brush down at that end of the garden, waited till Lutterbank had stormed out the gate, and then a few minutes later, she and Garrett McGraw scarpered off as well. Wesley says he watched Garrett put the girl in a cab.'

'Perhaps that's when she went to the Everdenes,' Betsy suggested. 'Maybe she didn't go right away, like she told Luty. Maybe when they give Mary the position, they told her not to come back till that evenin'.'

'No.' Mrs Jeffries shook her head, her expression thoughtful. 'I don't think so. Why would Mary lie to Luty about such a trivial matter? If the Everdenes had instructed her not to come till the evening, why not simply ask Luty for permission to spend the afternoon in Luty's home? And we know she never asked. She told Luty as soon as she returned from the agency that she had the position, and then she left immediately. But obviously, despite what the Everdenes claim, Mary was not in their home that night, but back in Knightsbridge. How very curious.'

'Maybe she was too proud to ask Luty to let her stay for the rest of the day,' Betsy continued doggedly. 'Luty did say that she was ever so proud.'

'I suppose that's possible,' Mrs Jeffries agreed reluctantly. She noticed that Betsy's chin was tilted in a determined angle as the girl glared at the grinning coachman. She had the distinct impression that Betsy was arguing more in an attempt to wipe that smug expression off Smythe's face than for any other reason.

'But it's not bloomin' likely,' Smythe retorted. 'Look, why should she fib to Luty about a piddlin' little matter like what time she were expected at the Everdenes? Besides, we've only got their word for it that she even turned up at all.'

'Are you suggestin' she never went to the Everdene house?' Betsy snapped.

'I'm sayin' it's possible,' Smythe argued. 'We've only got their word fer it that she showed up, and then they claimed she up and quit the very next day. If you ask me, that story sounds like a load of codswallop. The truth of the fact is the last time anyone really saw Mary Sparks was the evening of the tenth.'

'That's the silliest . . .' Betsy sputtered.

'It's not silly, it's a ruddy fact,' Smythe interrupted huffily.

'Yes, of course it is.' Mrs Jeffries said quickly. She smiled at Betsy. 'Now let's not argue among ourselves. Smythe does, indeed, have a point. Until we get assurances from someone other than the Everdenes that Mary was at their home on the tenth, we must assume that the last time she was seen was in the gardens on the afternoon of the tenth.'

Betsy gave Smythe one final glare. 'Oh, all right,' she muttered ungraciously.

Mrs Jeffries turned to the coachman. 'I expect you know what I want you to do next.'

He nodded. 'You want me to find that hansom driver and see if he took her to the Everdenes' or to some place else?'

'That's correct.' Mrs Jeffries turned back to Betsy. 'Now, what did Cassie Yates tell you about Mary?'

'Not much o' anythin',' Betsy admitted sheepishly.

Smythe smiled and said caustically, 'Couldn't get her ta talk, huh?'

'Fat lot you knows about it,' she retorted. 'I can git anyone to talk. But you can't get someone to chattin' if'n they's disappeared, can you?'

'Cassie Yates has disappeared too?' Mrs Jeffries asked in alarm. 'Oh dear, this is getting most complicated . . .'

'Don't fret yourself, Mrs J,' Betsy said soothingly. 'From what I heard about Cassie Yates, she can take care of herself. I talked to one of the girls that works in the shop with 'er, and she reckons Cassie's run off with some man. Says the girl had a couple of gentlemen friends and that she was goin' around braggin' about how both of 'em wanted to marry her. One of 'em had even posted the banns and bought the licence.'

Mrs Jeffries nodded. 'Did you find out where Miss Yates lives?'

'No. But I did find out she used to work for the Lutterbanks too. That's how her and Mary become friends.'

'Did they sack her?' Mrs Goodge asked.

'She quit about two weeks before Mary disappeared.' Betsy gave Mrs Jeffries a puzzled frown. 'Why'd you want to know where Cassie lives?'

'Because this case seems to be getting complicated,' Mrs Jeffries replied. She was hedging. Betsy was no doubt right and Cassie Yates was probably a respectable married woman by now. But she couldn't get the thought of Inspector Witherspoon's body out of her mind. She wasn't certain the dead girl was Mary Sparks or Cassie Yates. A coincidence like that would be odd, but not unheard of. However, until both young women were accounted for, she wanted as much information as she could get.

'What about me?' Wiggins scratched his chin. 'I found out quite a bit meself yesterday.'

Mrs Jeffries smiled at his enthusiasm. 'Were you able to find Garrett?'

'I found 'im all right, but I didn't have a lot of luck gettin' much out of the lad,' Wiggins reported sadly. ''E was right friendly-like until I mentioned Mary's name. Then 'e got all nervous and twitchy, kept lookin' over his shoulder like he was expectin' someone to be sneakin' up behind 'im and listenin'. It were right peculiar if you ask me.' He broke off and glanced towards the cupboard. 'Is there any of them currant buns left? I could fancy a bite or two.'

'The buns is all gone. When we've finished here, I'll get you a roll.' Mrs Goodge rolled her eyes. 'Now get on with it, boy. What did Garrett say?'

'Give us a minute. I'm gettin' to that.' He stopped and took a deep breath. ''E says he don't know Mary very well, just enough to speak to her every now and again in the garden, and that 'e ain't seen her since she left the Lutterbanks. But 'e also told me the Lutterbanks were a right nasty bunch, too. Fiona, that's the daughter, likes to tell tales, and Andrew, that's the son, is a bit o' a bully. Mrs Lutterbank, who used to be just a little on the barmy side, is now completely round the bend, and Mr Lutterbanks has a bad temper. Anyways, as soon as Garrett started talkin' about them, I asked him about Mary stealin' the brooch.' Wiggins paused dramatically. 'That's when 'e got angry. Claimed Mary Sparks wouldn't steal nothin' if her life depended on it, claimed the Lutterbanks were makin' up tales and they ought to be horsewhipped. He got right worked up, went on and on about it.'

'For someone who claimed not to know Mary very

well,' Mrs Jeffries said thoughtfully, 'he certainly leapt to her defence quickly enough.'

'That's what I thought,' Wiggins exclaimed.

'I think we need to keep our eyes on Garrett,' she continued. 'Wiggins, why don't you try and follow him this evening when he leaves work? See where he goes, find out where he lives and find out where his older brother lives.'

'Huh? Older brother?' Wiggins looked thoroughly confused. 'What's he got to do with it?'

Mrs Jeffries shrugged. 'Possibly nothing. But Luty Belle mentioned that Mary was almost engaged to Mark McGraw. He's away at sea. However, if he doesn't live with his family, he may have rooms somewhere and Mary may have taken refuge there. Especially if she could convince Mark's landlady she was his intended bride. It's a tad farfetched, I'll admit, but it's worth looking into.'

Smythe and Betsy started to get up, each of them eager to get on with their investigating. The housekeeper waved them back into their chairs. 'Don't go just yet. I'm afraid there's another matter we need to discuss.'

She then proceeded to tell them about Inspector Witherspoon's newest case. As was her custom, she told them every little detail she'd managed to wheedle out of the inspector.

'You don't think the body they found is Mary, do you?' Betsy's eyes were as big as saucers.

'It's possible. But whoever the victim is, I hope you understand what this means.'

'It means we've got two mysteries to solve.' Smythe

37

grinned wickedly. 'Blimey, it's either feast or famine around 'ere. When are we going to 'ave time to get our work done? I can't neglect them horses forever.' Smythe was absolutely devoted to the inspector's two horses, Bow and Arrow.

'Leave off with you, Smythe,' Betsy said. 'We'll have plenty of time for everythin'.' She grinned at the footman. 'Except for poor Wiggins here. He might have to cut back on his courtin' some.'

'I'm not courtin',' Wiggins said indignantly.

''Course he's not courtin',' Mrs Goodge teased. 'He's pinin'. There's a difference, you know. That pretty little maid from up the road hasn't looked his way once. She struts by with her nose in the air while the poor lad worships her from behind the drawing-room curtains.'

'I never,' Wiggins yelped. He blushed a bright pink. 'I was washin' them windows. Besides, Sarah Trippet isn't my sort of girl at all. She's too short.'

'Maybe that's why she's always walkin' about with her nose in the air,' Smythe suggested. 'She wants to look taller.'

Betsy and Mrs Goodge both laughed. Wiggins's infatuations were legendary.

Inspector Witherspoon's day was going from bad to worse. He stood over the trench where the body had been buried and shook his head. 'Are you absolutely certain, Barnes?'

'Absolutely, sir,' Constable Barnes said. 'These houses were vacant for months before they got around to tearing them down. The family that lived here was long gone before that body was buried. And you heard the police surgeon. He's fairly sure that with the amount of decomposition, the girl'd only been here for no more than two months. The folks that lived here has been gone for four.' He turned his head, frowning at the high wall on the other side of Magpie Lane. 'For that matter, so's everyone else. That brewery's been abandoned for almost a year now. We'll not be having any witnesses on this one, sir.'

'Drat.' Witherspoon glared at the one remaining house on the road. 'Why haven't they torn that one down yet?'

'They forgot.'

'They what!'

'They forgot it,' Barnes explained. 'According to the clerk at Wildworth's, that's the property company that owns this land, they forgot there was one house left to be demolished. But that's a bit of luck for us, sir. Mr Raines, the shopkeeper on the main road, claims there's an old man who dosses down in that house. If we can find him, he might be able to help us with our inquiries.'

'Excellent, Barnes. Get some men on it right away.' Witherspoon started towards the house.

'Yes, sir. Where are you going, sir?' Barnes called.

'To search that house,' Witherspoon replied. 'We've already searched this area, and we haven't come up with a thing.'

'But, sir. The men have already gone through it. They found nothing but the usual rubbish. Why are you going to do it again?'

Witherspoon hated to admit it was because he couldn't think of anything else to do. 'One never knows, Barnes,' he called out briskly. 'Perhaps I'll spot something the chaps have overlooked.'

Mrs Jeffries waited patiently at the top of the stairs for the rag-and-bone man to finish his tea. She didn't want to intrude on Mrs Goodge when she was pumping one of her prime sources for information. There was a regular stream of visitors to the kitchen at Upper Edmonton Gardens. Delivery boys, chimney sweeps, carpenters, and last week, there'd even been a man from the gas works chatting with Mrs Goodge as if they were old friends. But Mrs Jeffries didn't mind. Mrs Goodge was quite good at prying every tidbit of gossip out of those that passed through her kitchen.

Mrs Jeffries had no doubt that right at this very moment the cook was working furiously to find out anything she could about the Lutterbanks and the Everdenes. She sighed and leaned against the banister. Such a pity, really. So many in the upper classes failed to notice that many servants were diligent, perceptive and often highly intelligent human beings. Sad really, but so many of the wealthy were most indiscreet in both word and deed in front of those they considered beneath them. But then again, Mrs Jeffries concluded, if they actually treated servants and working people like human beings, no doubt she and the household would find helping the inspector a great deal more difficult. Mrs Jeffries supposed one could see that as the silver lining around the dark cloud that society cast on most of the city's population. It wasn't much of a comfort, but she decided it would have to do. The world was changing, that was for sure. But a fair and equitable way of life for all people certainly wouldn't happen in her lifetime. Still, she had great hopes that it would happen eventually.

She heard Mrs Goodge say 'Cheerio, ducks' to the rag-and-bone man and then the sound of the kitchen door closing. Mrs Jeffries flew down the stairs and into the kitchen.

Neither of the women wasted any time on preliminaries.

'I've got an interesting bit of gossip about the Everdenes.' Mrs Goodge smiled triumphantly.

Mrs Jeffries knew better than to ask the cook for her source. It could have been the rag-and-bone man who had just left, or it could have been any one of half a dozen other people. Mrs Goodge was nothing if not thorough. But the housekeeper was disappointed. She'd been hoping for a bit of information about the Lutterbanks. 'Indeed. How very enterprising of you, Mrs Goodge.'

'There's tea on the table, Mrs Jeffries.' Mrs Goodge waved a hand at the pot and moved her large bulk towards a chair. 'If you'll pour us a cup, I'll tell you everything.'

'It will be my pleasure.' She sat down and poured out two cups of the steaming brew. Handing one to the cook, she gazed at her expectantly.

'Well, it seems the Everdenes are from an old Yorkshire family. But there's only the reverend and his daughter left. Their branch never had much money until recently, when the girl inherited a packet from a distant relative. And a good thing it was too. But that's not the interestin' bit.' Mrs Goodge paused and took a quick sip of tea.

Mrs Jeffries curbed her impatience. It did no good to try and hurry the woman along. She would have her moment of glory.

'The Reverend Everdene left his last congregation under a cloud.' The cook smiled knowingly. 'And us bein' a bit more worldly than most, I reckon's you can guess just what kind of a cloud I'm referrin' to.'

Mrs Jeffries could. 'Choirboys or young women?'

Mrs Goodge pretended to look scandalized. Then her broad face broke into a grin. 'Young women. According to what I've heard, he used to limit his attentions to servants. But he made a mistake with the last one, and his hands got a bit too free with the daughter of the local magistrate. Naturally the church tried to hush up the scandal. But it ended with the Reverend Everdene out of Yorkshire and supposedly retired.' She broke off and cackled with laughter. 'It's a nice piece of luck his daughter inherited all that money. He didn't get another parish.'

'Hmm,' Mrs Jeffries said thoughtfully. 'That may explain why Mary Sparks left the Everdene house so precipitously. If the reverend tried . . . well, anything, she may have felt justified in leaving her post without notice. If, of course, she was there in the first place.'

'Humph. The old goat should be locked up. And him with a daughter too. He ought to know better.' Mrs Goodge pursed her lips. 'Disgusting. I feel sorry for the daughter, but at least she'll be gone soon. She's engaged to be married.'

'But that still leaves us in the dark,' Mrs Jeffries said thoughtfully. 'We still don't know for sure if Mary was ever at the Everdene house.'

'True. But if she was, we've at least got an idea of what made her leave so quickly. The old fool probably tried to start pawin' at her the minute she got there.'

'That's possible. I suppose the next step is to find out if Mary did or did not arrive at the Everdene house at all.' Mrs Jeffries cocked her head to one side. 'Mrs Goodge,' she said thoughtfully. 'If you were a young woman in genuine fear of being ravished, what would you do?'

'Do?' The cook snorted. 'I'd pack me things and get out of that house. And I'd be quick about it too.'

'But we know Mary hadn't much money. If she were frightened and desperate, where would she go?'

'I'd go to the one person who'd shown me a bit of kindness,' Mrs Goodge said promptly.

'Luty Belle Crookshank.' Mrs Jeffries shook her head. 'But Luty Belle was in Venice and the house was locked up.'

'There's ways of gettin' into locked houses. There's ways of gettin' into locked gardens too. Remember, it were still early September. Even if Mary couldn't get into Luty's house for shelter, she'd probably feel safer sleepin' in the communal gardens than she would walkin' the streets. And the Everdene house is in Putney. It's not close, but it in't that far neither.'

'Do you think she would have walked?' Mrs Jeffries sipped her tea.

'No. London streets are dangerous. If she'd had any money at all, she'd have taken a hansom.'

'I think you're right. And I think I'd better go have a nice little chat with Garrett McGraw.'

'The gardening boy?' Mrs Goodge looked puzzled. 'Why?'

'Because Mary knew that Luty was already gone. The only other friend she had was Garrett. If she crept back to Knightsbridge and hid in those gardens, it was for one reason and one reason only. She thought she could get help from someone.'

'But we don't know that she did any of that.'

'No, but I've got to start somewhere.' Mrs Jeffries rose to her feet. 'And in all fairness, I must tell Luty Belle about the body in Magpie Lane.'

CHAPTER THREE

L UTY BELLE WAS pacing the drawing room when
Mrs Jeffries arrived. 'Mornin', Hepzibah,' she said.
She gestured towards the settee, indicating that her
guest was to sit down. 'I've been expectin' you.'

'But you only came to see us yesterday,' Mrs Jeffries exclaimed as she settled herself comfortably on the
plush velvet cushions. 'Surely you don't imagine we've
found Mary so quickly.'

' 'Course not. But I knowed you'd have found somethin' out by now.' Luty sank wearily into a seat next
to the settee, her bright orange skirts clashing hor-
ribly with the deep red of the overstuffed wing chair.
'And you bein' the kind of woman you are, I knowed
you wouldn't waste any time tellin' me what you've
learned.'

Mrs Jeffries could see she was very worried. There
was a decided slump to her shoulders and deepening
lines of worry around her black eyes and thin lips.

'We've learned several interesting things,' Mrs Jeffries began briskly.

Luty's face brightened. 'I knowed I could count on

you,' she said earnestly. 'I knowed you'd come up with something!'

'First of all, we've learned that Mary came back here the day she was supposed to have gone to the Everdenes. She was seen in the gardens on the evening of the tenth. A witness saw her get into a hansom cab.'

'But that don't make no sense,' Luty said. 'Why'd she come back here after she'd gone to all that trouble to git that danged job?'

'We're not sure. Are you sure that your butler's information is correct? Are you absolutely certain he actually went to the Everdenes' home and enquired after Mary?'

' 'Course I'm sure. Hatchet's got no reason to lie. He might be an old stuffed shirt, but he does what I tells him. If he says he went there, then he did.' Luty shook her head. 'And they told him that Mary had come that day, worked the one evenin' and then left.'

'Hmm, yes. Then obviously, either we have a case of mistaken identity here or someone is not telling the truth.'

'Well, I know it ain't Hatchet,' Luty said. 'Why'd you think Mary come back? She was mighty anxious to git away from here. Kinda give me the idea she wanted to put plenty of distance between herself and the Lutterbanks.'

'She may have had equally good reason for wanting to put some distance between herself and the Everdenes,' Mrs Jeffries said. 'We don't know that she didn't go there and then decide to leave. There are some that say that the Reverend Everdene isn't an honourable man.'

Luty's lips curled in disgust. 'Couldn't keep his hands

46

to himself, eh? Mary wouldn't put up with bein' pawed by the likes of Andrew Lutterbank; I don't reckon she'd put up with it from some preacher either. That might explain why she hightailed it back here. Maybe she was hopin' I hadn't left yet.'

'Did she know what time you were leaving?'

'Yup. All the servants except Hatchet left right after breakfast. Mary was still here then, but she knew I were fixin' to be on the noon train. She left at nine o'clock, after she'd helped me do a bit o' packin', and Hatchet and I left for the station about eleven-fifteen.'

'Is it possible she came back, hoping to get into the house and stay here until you returned?' Mrs Jeffries asked.

'Don't reckon so,' Luty said slowly. 'Mary helped Hatchet and me lock this place up tighter than a floozie's corset early that mornin'. She'd a had to break out a window or knock down a door to git in, and I knowed she wouldn't do somethin' like that no matter how desperate she was.'

'Do you think she came back to get help from Garrett McGraw?'

'Maybe,' Luty said doubtfully. 'Like I told ya yesterday, Garrett was right sweet on Mary. But I'm purty sure that Mary has an understandin' with Mark McGraw. Too bad Mark's at sea. He'd a made danged sure that no one was botherin' the girl. But he ain't even due back in the country for another week or two, so he couldn't a taken Mary in. And I don't rightly see why she'd come to git help from Garrett. Ain't nothin' he could do.'

'Perhaps he sent her to his home?' Mrs Jeffries

suggested. 'The witness said Garrett put her into a hansom cab.'

'Nah,' Luty said. 'The McGraws are as poor as church mice. Mark sends money home whenever he can, but it don't go very far when you've got seven mouths to feed. Mr McGraw was hurt in a bad accident a couple of years ago and ain't worked since, so they's in a bad way. Garrett knows how hard life is for his family. He wouldn't be sendin' Mary there for them to feed and house.' She broke off and stared morosely at the far wall for a few seconds. Then she added, 'It don't look good, does it, Hepzibah?'

'It looks better than it did yesterday,' Mrs Jeffries replied. 'At least we're beginning to put together Mary's movements. Smythe is trying to track down the driver of the hansom that picked Mary up, and Betsy is trying to trace her friend, Cassie Yates.'

'Why you lookin' for her?' Luty snorted. 'Cassie ain't the kind to be takin' someone in.'

'Yes, but you did say she and Mary were friends. We're hoping Cassie Yates may have some idea of where Mary could have gone.'

'I don't think so. The only reason they was friends was because Mary felt sorry for her. Cassie was such a cat the other girls couldn't stand her.'

'But we're assuming that Mary was desperate,' Mrs Jeffries explained. 'We've heard that Cassie may have got married recently. If she's a respectable married woman, there's a chance that Mary may have gone to her to stay until you returned from Venice.'

'Cassie Yates a respectable married woman!' Luty laughed. 'That's danged unlikely.'

'Why ever not?'

'I don't know what kinda tales you been hearin', but Cassie Yates ain't the type o' woman to tie herself down to jest one man. Why at least twice, I've seen the little tart with men, and they wasn't jest talkin' neither, if'n you take my meanin'. One time she was letting Andrew Lutterbank kiss her, and the other time she was behind that big old oak tree with a blond-haired young feller, and they wasn't havin' tea together. Besides, if'n Mary went to Cassie, then why ain't I heard from her?' Luty jumped to her feet and began to pace the room. 'Even if'n Cassie'd take her in, and that's a big if'n, believe me, that don't explain why she didn't contact me when I come back. Mary knew when I was comin' home.'

Mrs Jeffries lowered her gaze and stared at the scrolling pattern of acanthus leaves in the Brussels–weave carpet beneath her feet. She had no choice. She had to tell Luty about the body. Despite her assurances to Betsy and the others, there was a chance that the corpse was the remains of Mary Sparks. Luty had a right to know.

'Luty,' she said softly, 'there's something else I must tell you.'

Luty stopped pacing. 'What?'

'There's been a murder. They've found the body of a young woman. She was wearing a dark blue dress. Inspector Witherspoon says the girl's been dead several months.'

The elderly woman stiffened and seemed to brace herself. 'Do you think it's Mary?'

'No. But I had to tell you. The possibility does exist. The timing is too coincidental to ignore. Besides that,

49

the deceased had dark blonde hair and a silver brooch was pinned on the lapel of her dress.'

For a moment, Mrs Jeffries thought Luty might faint. She watched her close her eyes, sway gently to one side, clutch the back of the chair and then take one deep, shuddering breath. 'Are you all right?' she asked in alarm.

Luty's eyes flew open and she straightened her spine. Ignoring Mrs Jeffries's question, she hurried to the door and flung it open. 'Hatchet,' she bellowed. 'Bring me my hat and cane.'

Puzzled, Mrs Jeffries leapt to her feet. 'What are you doing?'

'What does it look like? I'm gittin' ready to go out.' Luty took her hat and cane from the tall, white-haired butler, nodded her thanks and jammed the hat on her head. 'They've got the body somewhere, don't they?'

'Yes, of course they do,' Mrs Jeffries replied. 'Oh, no. You're not going to . . .'

'Yup. I wanta see it. I wanta see with my own eyes if it's Mary.'

'But, Luty,' Mrs Jeffries protested. 'According to Inspector Witherspoon, the body is so . . . so . . .'

'Rotten.'

'Decomposed.' She smiled gently, trying to think of a way to dissaude her friend from such a gruesome undertaking. There was no point in going to identify the remains if they were in no state to be identified. Luty would only upset herself. 'The inspector says it's impossible to tell who the woman was. You won't be able to tell whether that unfortunate young girl was

Mary or not. For goodness' sake, Luty, you'll only distress yourself.'

'Fiddlesticks, Hepzibah.' Luty scurried to the door. 'I've seen plenty o' corpses in my time, and ain't none of them ever sent me into a faint or caused a hissy fit. Now, come on, let's git this done. The sooner's we git there, the quicker we'll know that it ain't Mary.'

Mrs Jeffries hurried after her.

Hatchet, who Mrs Jeffries assumed was used to his employer's eccentricities, had already hailed them a passing hansom by the time they stepped outside.

Mrs Jeffries instructed the driver to take them to Scotland Yard.

'You will be careful, madam,' the butler said as he helped them into the cab.

'Ain't I always, Hatchet?'

'Not that I've noticed, madam,' he informed her as he slammed the door shut and nodded to the driver.

Luty settled back in the seat and grabbed the handhold to steady herself as the driver cracked the whip and the horses trotted forward. 'Where'd they find the body?'

'In the cellar of a torn-down house,' Mrs Jeffries answered. 'On Magpie Lane. That's in Clapham. All the houses had been torn down to make way for a new road, but then they changed their minds. They ended up digging instead, supposedly for one of those new underground railway lines.'

Luty made a face. 'Horrid things. Trains is bad enough. Fancy those fools thinkin' that anyone would want to ride one that went underground.' She faltered and her brows came together. 'Magpie Lane. Now, where have I heard that name before?'

'You've heard of it?' Mrs Jeffries asked. 'When? Where?'

'Offhand, I don't rightly remember. Give me a minute now.'

'Think, Luty. It may be important.'

'Why? I've heard of lots of places.'

'Because this street wasn't occupied by gentry or anyone else you're likely to have met. The homes that were torn down were all small houses let by the month. If you've heard the name before, there's a good chance that Mary had too.'

'Nells bells,' Luty said disgustedly. 'It went plum out of my head.' She held up her hand. 'Don't worry, Hepzibah, it'll come back to me. Just give me a few minutes to clear my mind.' She turned and stared out the open window. Luty remained silent as the cab rumbled up Knightsbridge and past Hyde Park. Mrs Jeffries was deep in thought as well. The hansom rolled on through the busy streets, and she jumped when Luty finally spoke.

'It were at that silly garden party last August.'

'What was?'

'Magpie Lane. That's where I heard the name. Emery Clements was complainin' about it.' She gave another inelegant snort. 'He kept goin' on about how his solicitors had evicted the tenants too early. Said the houses was all sittin' empty when they could have been collectin' rent.'

'Who gave the party? Who was there?' Mrs Jeffries noticed they were drawing close to Charing Cross. They'd be at the Yard soon.

Luty rubbed her chin. 'The Lutterbanks. They was

the one's giving it. That caused some talk too, seeing as how they was all supposed to still be in mourning for old Angus Lutterbank. He'd only died the month before. Not that I blame them fer not wastin' too much time grievin' for Angus – he was a nasty ol' fool. Had so few friends and neighbours willin' to come to his funeral service that the Lutterbanks made all their servants go jest to fill up the pews.' She snorted. 'But the place still looked half-empty.'

'Please, Luty,' Mrs Jeffries interrupted. 'About the party?'

'Oh, sorry. Anyways, like I was sayin', they had this here party and invited most of us that lives round the gardens, but they're such miserable people, most folks didn't come. Let's see. The Lutterbanks were all there, including Andrew and his sister, Fiona. I remember because Andrew kept gabbing at the maid serving the sandwiches. And they had two of their friends with them. Emery Clements, he was the one doin' all the braggin', and another young feller named Malcolm Farnsworth. There was others there too, but I'll have to think awhile to remember their names.'

'Was Mary there?'

'No. Mary was never anywhere near Andrew if she could help it.'

Mrs Jeffries leaned forward as the cab drew to a halt. 'Was anyone else nearby? Any other neighbours or servants?'

The cab stopped, and the driver leapt down and helped the ladies out. Luty handed the man a few coins, ignored his effusive thanks for the generous tip she'd included and grabbed Mrs Jeffries's arm.

'Garrett was weeding one of the flower beds,' Luty continued thoughtfully. 'And one of the other garden-ers was plantin' some early bulbs. I recall that because Mrs Lutterbank come out of her stupor long enough to yell at the boys to go work somewhere else. Well, I can tell you I told her quick enough that those boys were workin' where they'd been told to work and if'n she didn't like it, to take it up with the head gardener and not be shoutin' at them like they was dirt under her feet.'

'Yes, yes, I'm sure you did. Quickly, before we reach the inspector's office, tell me everything you heard about Magpie Lane.'

'All I heard Clements talk about was them houses bein' empty and him losin' his precious rent,' Luty replied as they climbed the steps and went inside.

'So every one of the people at the party knew that there were empty houses on Magpie Lane.'

'Yup. A body would've had to be deaf not to hear Clements's voice. He's louder than a mule with a burr under its blanket.'

Mrs Jeffries nodded and suddenly remembered something else. 'Why would Garrett be nervous to talk about Mary Sparks?'

Luty stopped abruptly. The uniformed constable behind the counter at the far end of the room stared at them curiously.

'I don't rightly know,' Luty replied slowly. 'There shouldn't be any reason for him to shy away from talk-ing about Mary. I could see him not wanting to talk about Cassie Yates, but exceptin' for him bein' a bit sweet on Mary, there ain't no reason for him to not want to talk about her.'

The constable came out from behind his desk and headed in their direction. Mrs Jeffries ignored him. 'Why would Garrett not want to talk about Cassie Yates?'

'Because that time she was bein' pawed behind the oak tree, well, Garrett happened to see it. He blushed so hard I was scared he was goin' to pass out from it.' She cackled. 'And we weren't the only ones to see her carryin' on either. Andrew Lutterbank was watching the whole thing from one of the upstairs windows. Come to think of it, it was right after that that Cassie left the Lutterbanks and went to work in that shop.'

Mrs Jeffries turned to the approaching constable and gave him a dazzling smile. 'Good morning, Constable. Could you direct us to Inspector Witherspoon?'

The mortuary at St Thomas's Hospital was one of Inspector Witherspoon's least favourite places. As he escorted the two ladies into the huge room, he tried not to wince. He loathed the peculiar trick of lighting that cast a faint, greenish glow on everything. Every time he set foot in this horrid place, he could feel the blood rushing from his head to his toes. He hoped he wouldn't become ill. It would simply be too embarrassing if he were to disgrace himself in front of Mrs Crookshank and his own housekeeper. He glanced at them out of the corner of his eye.

Both women were looking around the room with avid curiosity.

Dr Potter, who'd done the post-mortem on the body found in Magpie Lane, came forward to greet them. He was holding in his hand a dark red, wet object the size of a potato. Witherspoon cringed as the man paused next to a table and dropped the ominous-looking thing in a jar of liquid.

'What are you doing here, Inspector?' Dr Potter asked, smiling politely at the two ladies. 'I didn't expect to see you until the coroner's inquest.'

'Good day, Doctor.' Witherspoon tried not to breathe too deeply. The smell was appalling. 'I know the inquest isn't until the day after tomorrow. But as we already know we're dealing with a murder, we're not waiting until it's official before we start investigating.'

Potter's bushy black eyebrows rose. He was a heavy-set man of medium height, with thick black hair and a florid complexion.

'Allow me to introduce you to these ladies.' The inspector gestured to Luty. 'This is Mrs Crookshank, and this is my housekeeper, Mrs Jeffries.'

Dr Potter nodded politely.

'Mrs Crookshank would like to view the er . . . deceased,' Witherspoon explained hastily. 'She may be able to help in the identification.'

The doctor looked surprised. He turned to Luty Belle. 'You want to view the body, madam?'

'Unless you know of any other way I kin tell if'n it's Mary Sparks, I reckon I'll have to.' Luty gave him a long, hard stare.

'Mary Sparks?' the doctor repeated.

'That's a young friend of Mrs Crookshank's,' the inspector said. 'She'd like to ensure that the body isn't that of Miss Sparks.'

'But, madam,' Potter protested, 'I doubt you'll be

able to tell. The remains are in an advanced state of decomposition.'

'Why don't you let me be the judge of that? If'n it's Mary, I'll be able to tell, all right.'

Dr Potter wasn't used to having his judgement questioned. He drew himself up to his full height and fixed Luty with an intimidating glare. 'In my opinion, madam, I hardly think that's likely. The girl's own mother wouldn't be able to identify her. If you'd like, you may look at the victim's clothing. That may help tell who she was.'

'Dang and blast, man,' Luty cried in exasperation. 'This is no time for social niceties. I want to look at that corpse. It may be someone I know. I ain't squeamish and I ain't gonna faint, if'n that's what you're frettin' on.'

'Well, really,' Dr Potter said huffily. He turned and gestured towards one of his assistants, and the young man had to hastily wipe a wide smile off his face. 'If you insist, Dr Bosworth will take you into the morgue. Good day to you.'

'Oh, dear,' Witherspoon murmured. 'I believe he's offended.'

'Stupid fool,' Luty muttered. She marched behind the assistant like the Queen of Sheba. 'Men! What did the man expect me to do, faint or have a fit? It's a wonder the police ever git anyone identified. I've seen worse than anything they have here.'

As they walked down a long hallway, Luty kept up a long litany of various horrors and dead people she'd dealt with in her long life. By the time Bosworth ushered them through the door and into the morgue,

57

the poor young man's eyes were bulging. Mrs Jeffries noticed that Inspector Witherspoon had gone pale. Wanting to spare the doctor and the inspector further assaults on their sensibilities, she tugged on Luty's arm. 'Luty, please. You're making me quite ill.'

Luty broke off and stared at her suspiciously. She knew Hepzibah Jeffries wouldn't turn a hair over some of the things she'd been telling. Then she glanced at the inspector and the young physician. Seeing they were both pale, she nodded.

Bosworth gestured for them to come inside. They stepped into the dim, eerily quiet room. There were three tables, and on the centre one a shroud-draped corpse rested in silent dignity. As they walked farther into the room, Mrs Jeffries realized that the temperature was very low. She wondered how the hospital kept this room so cold.

'It's not a very pretty sight,' Bosworth warned as he drew back the covering. Mrs Jeffries steeled herself, Luty took a deep breath, and Inspector Witherspoon stepped back a pace.

The face was unrecognizable. Black, bloated and without colour, it could be identified as female only by the long blonde hair.

'Humph,' Luty snorted. 'The hair is the right colour, but I can't tell anything from looking at the face.'

Mrs Jeffries nodded. 'Did Mary have any distinguishing marks or scars upon her person?'

'Not that I know of.' Luty gestured for Bosworth to lower the covering. She turned to the inspector. 'Where's her clothes?'

Witherspoon, who was trying not to look at anything

except the floor, didn't realize that Mrs Crookshank was addressing him.

'He gone deaf or something?' Luty asked irritably when the inspector didn't reply.

'Inspector Witherspoon,' Mrs Jeffries said gently, 'Luty would like to see the victim's clothing.'

'Huh. Oh. Certainly. Uh, I believe they're . . .' He broke off because he didn't quite remember where they were.

Bosworth finally spoke up. 'They're still here. The police haven't taken them into evidence yet. We don't like to let them go until after the coroner's verdict.'

Witherspoon, who'd never heard of such nonsense, shook his head. 'All right, then. Go and get them. We'll wait, uh, well, out in the hallway.'

They moved into the corridor, and Witherspoon took several long, deep breaths of air. After a few seconds he began to feel better.

'How come they took her clothes off anyways?' Luty wanted to know. 'Seems downright disrespectful if you ask me.'

'Dear lady, nothing could be further from the truth,' Witherspoon assured her quickly. 'But the doctors can hardly determine causes of death if they can't examine the victims, and the only way to do that is to undress them.'

'Here's the victim's things, sir,' Bosworth said, handing a cloth bag to Inspector Witherspoon.

Gritting his teeth, the inspector put the bag on the floor and reached inside. He pulled out a tattered, dark blue dress with a silver brooch pinned to the lapel.

Luty Belle gasped. Then she reached over and lifted

59

the right sleeve. A small moan of distress escaped her as she studied the inside lining of the wrist.

'I take it the dress is familiar to you?' Mrs Jeffries said gently. Her heart went out to Luty. One look at the woman's face was enough to assure her that the dress had, indeed, belonged to Mary Sparks.

Numbly, Luty nodded her head.

'But how can you be sure?' Mrs Jeffries persisted.

Luty didn't answer right away. Her throat worked convulsively for a moment, and her breathing was harsh. 'Because I told her to sew this here little pocket into the lining.' She held the sleeve towards Mrs Jeffries. 'Mary didn't like to get out and about much. She was always scared of pickpockets and the like. Last summer, I showed her this old trick from when me and Archie used to hang about the Barbary Coast.' She blinked furiously to hold back the tears. 'See, the pocket's just big enough to hold a few coins. But Mary never carried more than a shilling or two.'

Witherspoon knew he should be relieved now that the body had been positively identified. But he felt awful. Poor Mrs Crookshank, despite her eccentricities, was dreadfully upset.

'There, there,' he said. 'Don't distress yourself, madam. You have my assurances that Scotland Yard will find the evil perpetrator that foully ended this young woman's life.'

Luty gave him an incredulous stare. Mrs Jeffries quickly said, 'Of course, Inspector. We have every confidence in the police.'

Witherspoon's chest expanded. Luty snorted.

'Now,' the inspector said. 'Why don't you take Mrs

Crookshank outside for a bit of fresh air? I wouldn't want to question her until she's quite recovered herself.'

'I ain't lost,' Luty interrupted, 'and you can ask me any questions you want. There's only one thing that's important now and that's findin' Mary's killer.'

'Are you going to keep the bag of clothes?' Bosworth asked. He was staring at Luty Belle in morbid fascination.

'Yes, yes. Of course I'm going to keep the clothes. This is evidence, man.' Witherspoon made a mental note to speak to Constable Barnes. The deceased's effects should have been taken into evidence at once.

'Luty,' Mrs Jeffries said. 'Can you identify the pin?' She pointed to the silver brooch.

'Yup. It's Fiona Lutterbank's all right, but I can't figure how it comes to be on Mary's dress.' She pursed her lips. 'I knows Mary didn't steal it.'

'Are you saying this brooch is stolen property?' Witherspoon asked curiously.

'According to Fiona Lutterbank it is.' Luty shrugged her shoulders. 'But I wouldn't believe her if she told me that dogs have fleas and cows eat grass. Girl's a god-awful liar. She probably gave Mary the pin and then told her father Mary stole it.'

'Oh, dear,' Witherspoon said. He didn't much like the way this was going. Mrs Crookshank didn't seem the type of lady who would stand back and let the police handle this murder in a tactful and diplomatic manner. He certainly hoped she wouldn't go about making wild accusations and calling people liars. That could make things most awkward. Most awkward, indeed.

'Are you absolutely certain that Mary didn't steal that brooch?' Mrs Jeffries wasn't sure why she was pressing the point, but her instincts were telling her it was important.

'Hepzibah. I'm a very old woman, and I've spent my life learning to judge a person's character. That's the only way you survive in a wild place like Colorado.' Luty crossed her arms over her chest. 'And I'm tellin' you, that girl was no thief. She'd have starved to death before she ever took something that didn't belong to her. I don't know whys that danged pin is on her dress, but I do know that however it got there, Mary Sparks didn't steal it.'

'But nonetheless, the pin is there.'

'Bosworth,' Dr Potter shouted from the other end of the corridor. 'Would you mind getting back to work?'

Bosworth started and then reluctantly excused himself. He continued to look longingly at the three of them as he trudged off.

'Now, now, Mrs Crookshank,' Witherspoon said. 'I don't question that you're an excellent judge of character, but sometimes even the best of us are fooled.'

The inspector refused to let go of the idea that Mary Sparks was a thief. Well, it would explain so very much. Yes, yes, he could see it now. No doubt Mary Sparks was part of a ring of thieves. Masquerading as a housemaid, she obtained positions in fine homes and took to stealing. There was probably a man in the situation as well, he decided. Someone she passed the goods on to. No doubt he'd stabbed her when she demanded a bigger share of the booty.

Luty glared at him. 'Speak for yurself, Inspector. I

ain't wrong about Mary. And if'n you're fixin' to pass her murder off as a fallin' out among thieves, you'd best just think agin.'

For one horrid moment, Witherspoon thought she'd read his mind. 'No, no,' he assured her quickly. 'I'm sure Miss Sparks was of the very finest character. You have my solemn word, madam. Regardless of the circumstances under which the unfortunate young woman was slain, I won't rest until her killer is brought to justice.'

'Humph.'

While Inspector Witherspoon and Luty Belle were sparring with each other, Mrs Jeffries was thinking hard. Her mind went over and over every scrap of information she and the other servants had come across. Luty was certain Mary wasn't a thief. So why was a stolen brooch pinned on the lapel of her dress? But perhaps Luty wasn't such a good judge of character after all. She slanted the woman a quick, assessing glance.

Luty had launched into a recitation of some of Scotland Yard's more spectacular failures. The inspector, much to his credit, was vigorously trying to defend the police force without offending his opponent.

Mrs Jeffries studied Luty's sharp, shrewd eyes. The American woman hadn't carved out a fortune in the ruthless wilds of the American West by being a fool. Therefore, she was inclined to accept Luty's assertion that Mary wasn't a thief. But if Mary hadn't stolen the brooch, who had? The murderer? And why pin it on her dress after she'd been killed?

'Inspector,' she said quickly, interrupting Luty's

63

tirade about the lack of gas-lighting fixtures in the poorer sections of London. 'Why don't you show Mrs Crookshank the betrothal ring? Perhaps she'll know something about it.'

'Huh.' Witherspoon blinked in surprise. 'Oh, yes.' He reached into the bag and fumbled for a moment before withdrawing the gold chain and the ring dangling on its end. 'Have you ever seen this, madam?'

Luty reached for the ring. She frowned as she studied it.

'Do you think Mark McGraw gave it to her?' Mrs Jeffries asked. 'You did say you thought the two of them had an understanding.'

'I've never seen it before,' Luty replied, handing it back to the inspector. 'But it don't look like anything Mark would have given her. It's awfully fancy.'

'What about the shoes?' Mrs Jeffries said. 'Perhaps you'd better show them to Luty as well. She may be able to tell you where Mary is likely to have bought them.'

Witherspoon dutifully dug into the bag once again and lifted out a pair of black high-topped shoes. Luty snatched them from his hand.

For several long minutes she stared at them. Then all of a sudden she started to smile. The smile turned into a chuckle, and the chuckle soon turned into a laugh. Within seconds, Luty was laughing so hard her whole body shook.

Witherspoon, thinking the woman had become so overwrought by the sight of Mary's shoes that she'd lost her mind, began to wring his hands. 'Oh, dear. Please, Mrs Crookshank. Do calm yourself.'

He turned to Mrs Jeffries. 'I knew this would be too much for her. Please, can't you do something? She's having hysterics.'

'She's not having hysterics, sir,' Mrs Jeffries replied. 'She's laughing.'

'I ain't never had hysterics in my life,' Luty protested as she brought herself under control. 'I was laughin' because this here pair of shoes is about the happiest news I've had in a month of Sundays.'

'What are you saying, Luty?' Mrs Jeffries stared at her friend curiously.

'I'm sayin' that that corpse I just looked at ain't who I thought it was.'

'You mean, now you're saying that the deceased isn't Mary Sparks?' If Witherspoon hadn't been so confused, he'd have been depressed.

'It sure as shootin' ain't.' Luty grinned. 'I don't know who that poor woman is, but I know who she isn't. She ain't Mary Sparks.'

Mrs Jeffries tilted her chin to one side. 'What leads you to that conclusion?'

Luty waved the pair of shoes under Witherspoon's nose. 'These shoes. They ain't Mary's. These clodhoppers are big enough to fit a bear. Mary's feet are small and dainty. They ain't much bigger than a child's. I knows because I was going to give her a pair of my old slippers last year when Mark was home. He was plannin' on takin' her on an outin' to Richmond Park. Now I've got right small feet for a woman my size, and my shoes looked like they was a couple of rowboats on Mary's tiny feet.' She cackled with glee. 'So that means that Mary's still alive.'

'Well, if Mary Sparks isn't the woman in there,' Witherspoon gestured towards the room they'd left earlier, 'who is?'

CHAPTER FOUR

Luty was in high spirits all the way home. Mrs Jeffries dropped her off in Knightsbridge and then proceeded on to Upper Edmonton Gardens. She'd changed her mind about having a talk with Garrett McGraw – there were a few more facts she needed before she tackled that duty.

As she'd expected, the household was gathered in the kitchen for the noon meal. Mrs Jeffries decided to wait until she heard their various reports before telling them that Luty Belle was certain the body discovered in Magpie Lane wasn't Mary Sparks.

She paused in the doorway and studied their faces. Smythe was hunched over his plate like a disgraced dog, Wiggins was shovelling rolls into his mouth as if he hadn't eaten in days, Betsy was smirking, and Mrs Goodge was staring out of the window with the intense concentration of a cat watching a sparrow.

Calling out a cheerful greeting, Mrs Jeffries crossed the room and took her seat at the head of the table. 'And how is everyone today?' she asked kindly, feeling that no matter how important the case, the niceties should be observed. Wiggins, Mrs Goodge and Betsy assured her they were all just fine. Smythe grunted.

Betsy tossed her blonde curls over her shoulder and shot the coachman a triumphant glance. 'Best let me go first this time,' she chirped happily. 'I expect I've got a bit more to tell than the others.'

Smythe gave her a quick glare but said nothing.

Obviously Betsy's enquiries had gone better than anyone else's, Mrs Jeffries thought as she filled up her plate. And the pretty maid wasn't being tactful about the fact either. But then she really didn't blame her. Smythe was hardly reticent about lording it over Betsy when he stumbled onto a particularly good bit of information.

'All right, Betsy,' she agreed. 'Do tell us what you've learned.'

'It was ever so interestin',' the girl responded eagerly. 'I went back to the shop and found out where Cassie Yates used to live.'

'Used to live?' Mrs Goodge interrupted. 'You mean she's not there now?'

Betsy shook her head. 'Her landlady told me she left two months ago. She had rooms in Morton Street, off the Brompton Road.' She wrinkled her nose. 'It wasn't a very nice place, but it's respectable. The landlady, Mrs Rose, claimed she didn't allow men up in the rooms or any other carryin's on. Said that Cassie didn't cause any trouble. She paid her rent on time and kept a civil tongue in her head.'

Mrs Jeffries was delighted that Betsy was taking care to pronounce her hs properly today. 'Did the landlady say where Cassie had gone?'

'She doesn't know.'

'Oh, dear,' Mrs Jeffries murmured. There was a sinking sensation in the pit of her stomach. She'd been so hoping that Betsy would report that Cassie Yates was alive and well. An image of the body she'd seen that morning lying in the mortuary flashed through her mind. 'That's rather bad news. I was hoping to hear that Miss Yates was now a respectable married woman.' Or even an unrespectable one living in sin, she silently added.

'But she is,' Betsy exclaimed. 'That's why Mrs Rose don't know where she's livin' now. She got married. Cassie weren't just braggin' when she claimed one of the men she'd been seein' actually wanted to wed her.'

Wiggins reached for another bread roll. 'Did you find out 'is name?'

'No, more's the pity. The only thing Mrs Rose could tell me was that he was tall and fair-haired. She claims she didn't get much of a look at his face – he 'ad on a top 'at and a scarf. She thought it were right funny, but the feller claimed he 'ad a bad cold and needed to keep the chill out.' She broke off and laughed. 'But Mrs Rose says he was a real gentleman. He dressed nice and carried himself well. He come and got all Cassie's things the day after they got married. Took 'em away in a hired carriage.'

'I don't suppose you managed to find out what day the gentleman came for his wife's belongings, did you?' Mrs Jeffries asked.

'Now, that's where I had a right bit of luck.' Betsy said with a grin. 'Mrs Rose remembered because he come on her daughter's birthday. It were September the eleventh. She was right irritated with 'im because she had to leave off in the middle of the noon meal and let 'im into Cassie's room. He tipped her 'alf a crown.'

'Very good, Betsy,' Mrs Jeffries said. The more excited the girl became, the worse her pronunciation. But that was understandable. She'd learned a great deal in a very short time. 'It's a pity Mrs Rose wasn't able to give you a better description of the man.'

'Yes, but like I said, all the woman saw of 'im was a bit of his 'air stickin' out from under his top hat . . . Oh yes, he had a funny hand too.'

'Funny hand?' Mrs Goodge repeated with relish. 'What'd you mean by that? Did he have webbed fingers? I knew a girl that had a hand like that. Worked for Sir Richard Morton out Richmond way.'

'It weren't webbed fingers,' Betsy replied impatiently. 'It might not be much of anythin' really. Mrs Rose said she thinks the man had a crooked little finger, only she in't certain. She only had a quick look when he was handin' her the coin.'

'Well, that's something at least.' Mrs Jeffries started to turn her attention to Smythe.

'But that's not all I've found out,' Betsy protested. 'The girls at the shop had plenty to say about Cassie too. Ellen Wickes, that's the one that seemed to be the best acquainted with her, says that Cassie quit her position a few days before she got married. Well, the manager was livid because Cassie was leavin' without givin' notice. He threw her out of the shop and told her never to come back. But Ellen claims she did come back.'

Smythe finally looked up from his potatoes and beef. 'Why?'

'To get the five shillings Ellen owed her. Ellen had been hopin' that Cassie had forgotten about the loan,' Betsy explained quickly. 'But she 'adn't, of course. Anyways, Ellen claims that Cassie showed up the day after she got her pay packet – that was on the mornin' of the tenth – and demanded her money.'

'What's so interestin' about that?' Smythe demanded. 'All it tells us is that Cassie Yates wasn't one to forget who owed her money.'

'If you'd just let me finish, you'd know.' Betsy straightened her spine. 'The money wasn't important. What's important is what happened when Ellen was tryin' to pay the woman. Ellen says she'd had to nip into the back room to get the coins, and when she come out, Cassie was runnin' out of the shop like the devil 'imself was on 'er heels. Ellen went to the door and saw Cassie chasing another girl around the corner. Well, whoever this girl was, she made Cassie forget all about the money. Ellen waited all day, but Cassie never come back.'

Mrs Jeffries frowned thoughtfully. 'Did Ellen see the other girl? Would she be able to tell us what she looked like?'

'No.' Betsy sighed. 'I asked her. All she could remember was seeing a bit of dark blue skirt disappearin' around the buildin'. She said it looked right funny. Cassie was wearing a fancy pink dress that had a bustle as big as a bread basket. The skirt was so tight she could barely walk, let alone run. Ellen had a right good giggle over that, watching Cassie tryin' to chase this girl without lifting her skirts too high. Not that Cassie wasn't the type to lift her skirts now and again, according to what Ellen was tellin' me . . .' Betsy broke off and blushed as she realized everyone was leaning forward and hanging on her every word.

Mrs Jeffries cleared her throat. 'Yes. Thank you, Betsy. Smythe, would you like to speak next?'

'Not much to tell,' the coachman muttered.

'I take it you weren't successful in tracking down the driver of the hansom?' Mrs Jeffries suggested. Really, she thought, Smythe was being awfully childish today.

He raised his dark brown eyes and gave her a long, level stare. Then he grinned. 'Successful? Well, I reckon that depends on 'ow ya look at it. I got a right earful of gossip about that funeral the Lutterbanks had a few months back. The blokes I was talkin' to had done the funeral drivin'. But none of them had picked up Mary Sparks on the night she disappeared.'

'What'd you hear, then?' Mrs Goodge leaned forward with an expression of avid interest on her broad face.

'Just that the family insisted all the drivers come inta the church for the service, paid 'em extra to do it, and the funny thing was, the only one doin' any cryin' at the funeral was one of the housemaids.'

'Yes, yes,' Mrs Jeffries interrupted impatiently. 'I'm quite certain that's all very interesting. However, we really must keep our minds on our current problem.'

Smythe flushed guiltily. 'Sorry. Like I was sayin', I ain't found the one that picked Mary up yet, but I will. One of the other drivers gave me the names of three men who were working the streets around the gardens that night. I've done talked to one of 'em, and he don't remember the lass, but I'm hopin' one of the other two will.' He rubbed his chin. 'Do you happen to know if Mary was pretty?'

Wiggins's eyes lit up.

'I'm assuming she must be,' Mrs Jeffries replied. 'Garrett McGraw's infatuation and the fact that Luty has implied that Mary had to fight off the unwanted attentions of Andrew Lutterbank lead me to assume she must be a most attractive young woman.'

'Good.' Smythe leaned back in his chair and fixed Betsy with a cocky grin. 'I like lookin' for pretty girls.'

'Me too,' Wiggins added.

Betsy and Mrs Goodge both snorted, and even Mrs Jeffries smiled before turning to the footman. 'All right, Wiggins, it's your turn. Did you follow Garrett McGraw after he left the gardens yesterday evening?'

' 'Course I did. But it didn't do no good. He just went home.'

'He didn't stop off anywhere?' Mrs Jeffries prodded. She'd rather hoped that young Garrett would lead them to Mary. He was the last person known to have seen her and therefore their only real clue.

'He didn't stop,' Wiggins answered. 'He went 'ome. I hung around outside a bit, but the only one who come out was one of Garrett's little brothers.'

Mrs Jeffries nodded. She looked expectantly at Mrs Goodge.

'Sorry,' the cook said, 'I ain't remembered anything about the Lutterbanks, but I've got me feelers out. Give me another day or two – I'll have a few bits and pieces by then.'

'Very well,' Mrs Jeffries said. 'I believe it's my turn now.'

73

The others sensed the change in her tone. Everyone's expression sobered as they gave her their full attention.

'This morning I told Luty Belle about the murdered girl,' Mrs Jeffries began solemnly. 'She insisted on going to the mortuary and viewing the body. It wasn't a chore I relished, but once Luty Belle Crookshank makes up her mind, there's no stopping her.'

'Ugh, how awful,' Betsy said sympathetically.

'Indeed, it wasn't very pleasant,' Mrs Jeffries agreed. 'But you'll all be pleased to know that despite the distastefulness of the task, we learned something very important. Luty's sure the body isn't Mary Sparks.'

'Thank the good Lord for that,' Mrs Goodge said.

'However, there is something else you should know.' Mrs Jeffries paused. 'Whoever the girl was, she was wearing Mary's dress, and the brooch that Mary had been accused of stealing from the Lutterbanks was pinned on the lapel.'

'Cor! Blimey, this is getting more confused by the minute.' Smythe scowled. ''Ow did this girl come to be wearin' Mary's clothes?'

'I don't know,' Mrs Jeffries replied earnestly. 'But obviously the two cases are now connected.'

Betsy grimaced. 'Did you see the body?'

'Yes. It wasn't a pretty sight. Frankly, it was unrecognizable. Luty Belle only realized it couldn't be Mary when she looked at the shoes. They were much too large to have belonged to her.'

'And didn't the inspector say they were new shoes?' Mrs Goodge said thoughtfully, remembering the details the housekeeper had shared with them earlier.

Mrs Jeffries gave her an approving smile. 'Yes. And

Mary Sparks had just lost her position. She'd hardly have gone out and bought a pair of new shoes. But Cassie Yates, on the other hand, was apparently not in the least concerned about making a living. She'd quit her position.'

Wiggins looked up from his now-empty plate and said, 'Do you think the dead girl is Cassie Yates?'

'I'm not sure. If Betsy's information is correct and Cassie got married, then it's highly unlikely she's the victim.'

'Now, why would the dead girl be wearin' Mary's clothes?' Betsy mused. 'And 'ow did she get them?'

'I don't know,' Mrs Jeffries said. 'But we're going to find out.'

'Hmmm? That's gonna be a bit 'ard. We'll need more luck than most is given to find out what 'appened to this one.' Smythe crossed his massive arms over his chest. 'Seems to me that all we know so far is that Mary Sparks got into a 'ansom and disappeared on the evening of the tenth. Supposedly, Cassie Yates got married that very same day, and an unknown woman wearin' Mary's clothes gets herself done in and buried in a cellar at around about this same time.'

'What are you getting at, Smythe?' Mrs Jeffries asked.

'I ain't sure. I just don't like the way this is startin' to look.'

Betsy leaned forward on her elbows. ' 'Course we don't know that the dead girl's got anythin' to do with either Mary or Cassie, but it's a bit too . . . too . . .' Searching for the correct word, she broke off.

'Coincidental,' Smythe supplied. Betsy gave him an irritated frown.

Seeing another tiff brewing, Mrs Jeffries hastily stepped into the discussion. 'You're absolutely right, Smythe, it is too coincidental. The first order of business is for you to find that cab driver. It's imperative that we trace Mary's movements.'

'Mary's movements?' Mrs Goodge echoed. 'Shouldn't we be lookin' for Cassie Yates too?'

'Of course,' Mrs Jeffries answered smoothly. 'But finding Mary is our most important task. That's why Wiggins is going to keep Garrett McGraw under observation from the time he leaves the gardens tonight until he returns there in the morning.'

'All night?' Wiggins wailed. 'But it's cold at night.'

'Stop frettin', boy,' Smythe interjected. 'I'll be along after the pubs close to relieve you.'

'The pubs!' Betsy screeched. 'You can't be goin' off for a drink when you're supposed to be findin' that driver.'

'Of course he isn't going out to drink, Betsy,' Mrs Jeffries said. 'I have no doubt that Smythe will find the driver we seek well before the pubs open.' She looked at Smythe. 'Right?'

'As usual, Mrs J.' He gave her a lazy grin and rose to his feet. 'I'm goin' to the stables now.' He started walking to the door and then suddenly stopped. 'Do you want me to see if I can find out where the carriage that took Cassie Yates's things was hired from?'

Smythe knew every stable and livery in the city. Mrs Jeffries was annoyed at herself for neglecting to think of that.

'Excellent idea.' She beamed her approval. 'Perhaps we'll get lucky. Perhaps the carriage was hired from Howards. That would certainly save you some time.'

Looking decidedly sceptical, he left. Howards was the stable where the inspector's carriage and horses were kept.

'What do you want me to do next?' Betsy asked eagerly.

Mrs Jeffries thought for a few moments. 'We need to concentrate on finding Cassie Yates. If she married, the marriage would be recorded in the parish church. Go back and talk to Ellen Wickes. If the wedding was held at any of the churches around here, she might know which is the most likely.'

Betsy nodded and stood up. 'But what if the banns were read at the groom's church?'

'That's a possibility. I tell you what, if you can't get any more information out of Ellen Wickes, why don't you see if you can make the acquaintance of anyone else who knew Cassie? Try her lodging house, and you might want to see if any of the other maids at the Lutterbank household would be able to give you any help. They may not have liked Cassie, but one of them may have known the name of her young man. Sometimes one's enemies are more inclined to talk than one's friends. Let's hope so anyway. As a matter of fact,' Mrs Jeffries added, 'try and get the names of any young men Cassie might have been involved with.'

Betsy arched an eyebrow. 'From what I've 'eard of 'er, that might be quite a list.'

'Just get the most recent ones,' Mrs Jeffries advised, refusing to be offended by Betsy's bluntness. When one was investigating a murder and a disappearance, one didn't cling to outdated and ridiculous notions about whether or not innocent young housemaids should be so knowledgeable about the more unsavoury aspects of the human condition. 'Concentrate on the men Cassie is likely to have known this past year.'

'I expect you want me to put a bit of a fire under some of my sources,' Mrs Goodge asked as she heaved herself out of the chair. 'The butcher's boy is due in a few minutes. I'll have him snoop around some . . . and ol' Horace, the fruit vendor, is due on the corner this afternoon. I 'aven't had a chat with 'im in a long time . . .' She picked up the teapot and wandered towards the pantry, muttering to herself as she walked.

Mrs Jeffries had no doubt that by this time tomorrow, Mrs Goodge would know every morsel of gossip or scandal about the Lutterbank family. She only hoped that there'd be something genuinely useful in the information.

As the housekeeper went about her duties, she went over and over the few facts they'd obtained concerning the missing girl and the body buried in Magpie Lane. By some bizarre twist of fate, the two cases were now linked. It couldn't be a coincidence that Emery Clements was the owner of the property company that owned those houses, and it would be equally unlikely that after he'd publicly complained about the houses standing vacant, a girl would be murdered and buried there by chance. Not when so many of the principals were directly connected to the Lutterbank house, and it was at a Lutterbank party that Mr Clements had voiced his displeasure over the vacant property and the lost rent.

After she'd checked the linen cupboards, Mrs Jeffries came downstairs. On the bottom step she stopped suddenly. Gracious, she thought, I'm overlooking one of the obvious courses of action. No one had gone back to the Everdene house. She pursed her lips as she remembered the rather ugly gossip Mrs Goodge had shared with her. Mary Sparks was a lovely young girl. Reverend Everdene had an unsavoury reputation.

Mrs Jeffries yanked off her apron and hurried to the hall closet for her cloak and hat. Taking time only to stick her head into the stairwell and tell Mrs Goodge she'd be back later, she snatched her reticule from the hall table and raced out of the door.

The Everdene house was a large grey monstrosity squatting at the end of a row of newer semi-detached redbrick villas. An expanse of shrubs, lawn and trees separated the house from its smaller neighbours. Mrs Jeffries, who'd walked from Putney High Street, took a deep, calming breath and boldly marched up the broad stone steps.

She banged the knocker and waited, hoping that the door would be answered by a nice, motherly-looking housekeeper. She'd considered her strategy on the way there and had decided things would go far more smoothly if she could gain the confidence of another woman. Preferably an older woman. Hopefully the housekeeper.

But the door wasn't opened by a nice friendly female. It was opened by an unsmiling, bald-headed butler. Mrs Jeffries immediately discarded her first plan and went to her second one.

'Good day,' she said firmly, drawing herself up to her full height of five foot three. 'I would like to speak to Miss Everdene.'

'Who shall I say is calling, madam?'

'I fear my name will mean nothing to your mistress,' Mrs Jeffries said. 'But my business is of the utmost importance. Please tell Miss Everdene I'm here concerning a missing girl.'

He looked faintly surprised. 'Wait here, please,' he said, stepping aside and gesturing for her to enter. 'I'll see if Miss Everdene is receiving.'

Mrs Jeffries was fairly sure Antonia Everdene would be willing to speak with her. Her assumption was correct, for a few moments later, the butler returned. 'Miss Everdene will see you.' He led the way down an oak-panelled hall to a set of double doors and nodded for her to enter.

Mrs Jeffries stepped inside. The drawing room was panelled in the same dark oak as the hall, and the windows were covered with heavy royal-blue curtains. Sitting on the settee next to the fireplace was a young woman. 'Miss Everdene?' Mrs Jeffries said politely.

'I'm Antonia Everdene,' the woman replied. She didn't smile or rise in greeting. She had mousy brown hair worn parted in the middle and drawn back in an unbecoming bun. Her features were narrow and sharp, her mouth a thin, disapproving line. Deeply set hazel eyes regarded Mrs Jeffries suspiciously for a few seconds; then Antonia lifted a hand and impatiently gestured for her to come forward. 'Who are you and what do you want?'

Mrs Jeffries smiled coolly. 'My name is Hepzibah Jeffries,' she said as she sat down opposite the woman. 'And as I told your butler, I'm here seeking information about a missing woman.'

Beneath Antonia Everdene's sallow complexion, she paled. 'I've no idea what you're talking about. I don't know why I told Piper I'd see you. You'd better leave.'

'I think not,' Mrs Jeffries said firmly. 'If you didn't have some idea as to why I was here, you'd have had your butler show me the door immediately. But you didn't. Therefore, I must assume you have some knowledge of her whom I seek. Please, Miss Everdene, let us speak plainly. I'm here to ask you some questions about a Miss Mary Sparks. And I'm not the first person to come and enquire about her either.'

'How dare you!'

'I dare because I must,' Mrs Jeffries explained patiently. 'Your home is the last place that Mary Sparks was seen.' She paused dramatically and added, 'Alive.'

'This is an outrage. We know nothing about a missing girl.'

Mrs Jeffries could see that the woman was on the verge of panic. She decided to try another tactic. Smiling kindly, she said, 'Miss Everdene, I assure you, I haven't come here seeking anything but your help. A young woman is missing. We fear she may have come to some harm.'

Antonia Everdene's beady hazel eyes watched her warily for a moment before she nodded. 'All right,' she said grudgingly. 'I don't see why I should speak with you, but as you're here, I may as well find out what this nonsense is all about.'

'As I said, it's about a young woman named Mary Sparks,' Mrs Jeffries answered, watching the other woman closely. Beneath her haughty demeanour, she could see the fear in Antonia's eyes. 'She came here about two months ago. On September the tenth.'

'I don't know anything about that. Mrs Griffith, my housekeeper, takes care of hiring the servants.' She gave a patently false shrug of her shoulders.

'You mean you never saw Miss Sparks,' Mrs Jeffries persisted, deliberately using the girl's name again. She wanted to impress upon Miss Everdene that a human being was missing, not an object or a piece of furniture. 'But surely that's impossible. Mary was here for at least one night. Someone in your household, possibly your housekeeper, has already admitted that much.'

'I didn't say I never saw the girl,' she snapped. 'But who pays attention to servants?'

'Didn't you see her when you interviewed her for the position?'

'All interviewing is done by either a domestic agency or my housekeeper. I don't like to be bothered.' Antonia Everdene's hands balled into fists. 'However, I did catch a glimpse of the girl the day I dropped into the agency to see how much longer it would take them to find me a maid. Miss Hedley pointed to a young woman who was just leaving and said she'd found someone for me and that the girl would be at the house later that morning. The only other time I saw this person was in the early evening, when she escorted my dinner guests into the parlour.'

She rose imperiously to her feet. 'The girl was gone before I awakened the next morning. For all I know, she may have left in the middle of the night. So you see, Mrs Jeffries, neither I nor my servants can help you find this person.'

Mrs Jeffries stayed seated. 'What was the girl you saw at the employment agency wearing?'

'Wearing?' she repeated, obviously surprised by the question. 'I don't know. It was two months ago, I hardly make it my business to remember what kind of dress a housemaid was wearing.'

'I suggest, Miss Everdene,' Mrs Jeffries said smoothly, 'that you try. I should hate to have to tell the police a vital clue in their inquiries couldn't be obtained because of your lack of recollection.'

The veiled threat hit its mark, and Antonia Everdene blanched and sat down again. 'Police? Who said anything about the police?'

'I did. You see, I'm afraid if I'm unable to obtain a little more information from you, I'll have to go to my employer and ask for his help.'

'Your employer? But you're not from the police. They don't have women police persons . . .'

'My employer is Inspector Gerald Witherspoon of Scotland Yard,' Mrs Jeffries said calmly. 'Mary Sparks is, shall we say, a friend of a friend. She's disappeared. We want to find her. If you can be of any help in finding this young woman, then I shan't have to bother Inspector Witherspoon. Otherwise . . .' She trailed off, letting the implication hover in the air.

'The girl was wearing a dark blue dress,' Miss Everdene said quickly. Her composure was slipping rapidly. She twisted her hands together in her lap, and the movement caused Mrs Jeffries to note the small gold ring she wore on her left hand. 'Naturally, once she was here, she changed into the proper housemaid's dress. But she was only here for one night.' Her voice rose. 'I don't see why you or anyone else should be worried about one such as her . . . Bold little baggage, she couldn't keep her eyes off my fiancé. Not that he would ever take notice of the impudent chit.'

Mrs Jeffries looked at her sharply. That hardly sounded like Mary Sparks. 'Are you saying that she flirted with your intended?'

'Flirted!' she replied in disgust. 'It was worse than that, she was positively shameless in her behaviour. When she helped him off with his coat, her hands were all over him. The brazen hussy simpered and smiled and coiled around him like a cat. She was so bold that even when she tore her eyes away and saw me standing in the doorway, she didn't stop. She just kept smiling and patting her hair and swaying her hips. It was disgusting.'

'I presume your fiancé was shocked by her behaviour?'

'Of course he was,' Antonia snapped. 'But Malcolm is a gentleman. He pretended not to notice that anything was wrong.'

'And what did you do about her behaviour?' Mrs Jeffries asked.

'Do?' Antonia's chin rose. 'I waited until Malcolm was talking with Father, and then I hurried into the pantry and told the little beast her behaviour was intolerable.' The words tumbled out quickly now. 'I told her I wasn't going to put up with that kind of insolence and for her to pack her things and be out of the house by morning—' She caught herself, and her hand flew to her mouth as she realized what she'd said.

'So Mary didn't leave unexpectedly. You sacked her.'

'Yes,' she hissed. 'Of course I sacked her. Her behaviour almost ruined what should have been the most important evening of my life. I was furious at her. I knew Malcolm was going to ask Father for his permission to marry me. I was right too, because as soon as I went back into the drawing room, Father announced that he'd give us his blessing.'

'Exactly when did your fiancé propose?'

'Why do you ask? What difference does it make?' Miss Everdene's eyes narrowed suspiciously.

'I was merely curious,' Mrs Jeffries said blandly.

'Well, if you must know, Malcolm had proposed to me the evening before. We were at the opera.'

'Malcolm? Is that your fiancé's name?'

'That's none of your concern,' Antonia snapped. 'My fiancé has nothing to do with that girl being missing.'

'Really?' Mrs Jeffries replied. 'I'd hardly say it had nothing to do with him. He was, after all, the reason you sacked Mary.'

'He can hardly be at fault because some silly maid took it into her head to flirt with him.'

Mrs Jeffries decided not to press the point. There were other ways to find out the man's name. 'True,' she agreed. 'What did Miss Sparks do when you told her her services were no longer needed?'

'The impudent girl laughed in my face.' Antonia Everdene's expression hardened.

'Did she say anything?' From the look on Antonia's face, Mrs Jeffries was sure the girl had said plenty.

Antonia bit her lip and stared at the carpet. 'No. She said nothing. She just turned and stalked off. I never saw her again. The next morning, she was gone.'

'Did she take her things with her?' Again, Mrs Jeffries decided not to press the point. She could easily find out what had passed between Miss Everdene and Mary Sparks another way. Knowing servants as she did, she was sure someone had overheard the exchange.

'Yes. She only brought one small carpetbag with her. It was gone the next morning as well, so I presume she must have taken it with her.'

'Did anyone see the girl leave?'

Miss Everdene shrugged. 'No, she obviously left the house before the rest of the servants had got up.'

'How did she get out, then?' Mrs Jeffries asked. She knew most households were locked up tighter than a bank vault.

'The key to the back door is kept on a nail in the kitchen. When the housekeeper and cook went in, they found the back door standing wide open and the key in the lock. Obviously, she got up early, let herself out and didn't bother to close the door.'

'I see.' Mrs Jeffries started to get up and then stopped. 'Did your father meet Mary Sparks?'

'No,' she replied quickly. Too quickly. 'No. Father was gone all afternoon. He might have caught a glimpse of her when she was answering the door, but he didn't really see her. When he came in that evening, he stayed in the study until Malcolm arrived. By the time we went in to dinner, the girl was in her room.'

Mrs Jeffries suspected this was a lie. But like the full name of the mysterious fiancé, she knew she could get the truth from easier sources. She made a mental note to send Smythe over to try the pubs in Putney.

Antonia Everdene got to her feet. Lifting her chin,

she said, 'I believe I've told you everything I know. If you'll excuse me, I've got an appointment with the dressmaker.'

The interview was clearly over. Mrs Jeffries smiled and rose as well. She said a polite farewell and turned on her heel. She could feel the other woman's gaze boring into her back as she left the drawing room and let herself out. She breathed a sigh of relief as the front door closed behind her, and then she hurried off down the road towards Putney High Street.

Mrs Jeffries caught an omnibus on the High Street. The interview with Miss Everdene had given her the most unexpected results.

As the omnibus trundled over the newly built Putney Bridge, which had only been completed two years earlier, in 1884, she gazed at the dark water of the Thames.

Antonia Everdene was frightened. But why? Sacking a servant, even if the servant did come up missing later, wouldn't explain the depth of fear she'd sensed in the woman. Unless, she thought, Miss Everdene knew a great deal more than she was willing to tell about Mary's disappearance. Or unless the lady suspected that someone else knew something they weren't telling. Someone, perhaps, that Miss Everdene was trying to protect.

CHAPTER FIVE

IT WAS MID-AFTERNOON when Mrs Jeffries arrived back at Upper Edmonton Gardens. Deep in thought, she climbed the steps. She felt sure she'd learned something vitally important from Antonia Everdene, but she wasn't sure what. She gave herself a small shake as she opened the door and stepped into the hall. There would be time enough to put all the pieces together later, she told herself firmly. As her dear late husband, who'd been a constable in Yorkshire for over twenty years, had always said, during the first days of an investigation, gathering as many facts as possible was the most important task. Making sense and drawing the correct conclusions about those facts should then follow as a matter of course. She mustn't try to rush things. Justice would be served in its own good time.

The house, save for Mrs Goodge, was deserted. Mrs Jeffries took off her cloak and hat and hurried down the hall and into the cupboard under the kitchen stairs. Arming herself with a feather duster and broom, she retraced her steps and started dusting the furniture and knick-knacks in the drawing room. When the other servants were out on the hunt, she frequently took it upon herself to do their work. Menial labour helped her think. Today she had much to think about.

Half an hour later the mindless, repetitive chores had worked their magic, and she'd decided what the next likely course in their enquiries should be. She put the duster and broom away, took off her apron and went in search of Mrs Goodge.

The fruit vendor and the butcher's boy were leaving by the back door as she came into the kitchen.

Mrs Goodge gave her a triumphant smile and said goodbye to her guests. As soon as the back door closed, she turned. 'Good afternoon, Mrs Jeffries. I'm glad you're back.'

'I take it your enquiries have been successful?'

'Very.' She nodded towards the white china teapot on the table. 'Do you have time for tea?' At Mrs Jeffries's nod, she picked up a cup and saucer from the sideboard.

'I'm not all that sure that I've learned anything useful about Mary's disappearance,' Mrs Goodge said honestly as she set the tea in front of the housekeeper. 'But you did tell me to find out what I could about the Lutterbank family, and that's what I've done.'

'We don't know yet what will or will not be useful,' Mrs Jeffries replied. 'So please don't worry about that. Just tell me what you've found out since I've been gone.'

'The Lutterbanks have lived in Knightsbridge for about five years,' Mrs Goodge began. 'They's originally from Leicestershire. The money comes from shoes. They own a factory up around Market Harborough way, so I wasn't able to find out what they was up to before they come to London.'

'But you were able to find out something?'

'Well, I had to dig long and hard to get the few bits and pieces I got today,' she said slowly. 'But I did learn one interestin' tidbit. Last year, there were some right nasty rumours about the son, Andrew.'

'What kind of rumours?'

'The usual ugly ones,' Mrs Goodge said in disgust. 'Seems he was havin' his way with a young housemaid. 'Course when the girl gets in trouble, Andrew didn't want to know. Not at first, that is.'

'Oh, dear. I suppose the poor girl lost her position.' Mrs Jeffries wasn't surprised. It was an age-old story.

Mrs Goodge nodded. 'The girl's the one that always suffers, isn't she? Especially them that's all alone, like this girl was. But it didn't work out too badly for the lass. She weren't tossed out in the streets. The butcher's boy heard the story from the tweeny that lived in the house next door to the Lutterbanks. There was quite a to-do about it all, because the girl went running to old man Lutterbank and claimed that Andrew had forced himself on her. Claimed she could prove it too.' She broke off and grinned. 'She must have been pretty convincing, or maybe the Lutterbanks wanted to avoid a scandal, because they paid the girl off and the next thing you know, she's gone to Australia.'

Mrs Jeffries looked surprised. 'By herself?'

'I'm not rightly certain.' Mrs Goodge pursed her lips. 'I reckon she must have gone on her own if she didn't have a family. Why?'

'Well,' Mrs Jeffries replied thoughtfully, 'I think

that it's very odd for a pregnant young woman to just up and sail off to a foreign country all by herself, don't you? If they gave her a settlement, why did she leave? Why not just go to another part of England? The trip to Australia is long and difficult under the best of circumstances, let alone for someone expecting a child.'

'Hmm, I hadn't thought of it like that,' Mrs Goodge admitted. 'It is a bit strange, unless she's got people there. Maybe some of her relatives had emigrated? There's been a lot that's gone, you know.'

'That could be the answer, I suppose,' Mrs Jeffries said. 'Did you find out the girl's name?'

'Hello, hello. Anyone home?' Witherspoon called cheerfully from the top of the stairs.

Mrs Jeffries leapt to her feet. 'Gracious, what's he doing home so early?'

'I hope he's not here to eat,' the cook mumbled darkly as the housekeeper raced out of the kitchen and up the stairs.

'Good afternoon, Inspector,' Mrs Jeffries said brightly. 'What are you doing home at this hour, not that it isn't a pleasure to have you here?'

'How good of you to say so,' Witherspoon replied with a broad smile. 'I do hope it isn't a nuisance, my popping in in the middle of the day, but I was just over on Holland Park Road and as I was so close by, I thought I'd come in for tea.'

'Why, not at all, sir,' she assured him. 'What were you doing on Holland Park Road? Anything interesting?'

'Oh, yes. Yes, indeed. We've finally had a spot of

luck on this wretched murder case. I was at Broghan's, the jewellers at the top of the hill. They're the ones that made the betrothal ring.'

'Goodness, sir, you certainly found that out quick enough.'

Witherspoon shrugged modestly. 'Just doing my duty, Mrs Jeffries, no more, no less.' He broke off and frowned. 'I say, the house is awfully quiet today . . .'

'Why don't you have your tea out in the gardens?' Mrs Jeffries said hastily.

'But won't it be a bit chilly . . . ?'

'Not at all, sir.' She raised her voice, hoping that Mrs Goodge would hear. 'I know it's November, but it's a lovely day outside. Pity to waste it.' She glanced over her shoulder and saw the cook's round face peeking up from the top of the stairwell. Mrs Goodge nodded, indicating she'd bring the tea outside.

'I say,' Witherspoon said as they seated themselves at one of the small wooden tables, 'this is a jolly good idea. It's most pleasant out here.'

'I thought you'd enjoy the view,' Mrs Jeffries replied. 'You've been working so very hard on this latest murder case, I thought perhaps a breath of fresh air might be just the thing.'

The garden was still lovely. The leaves on the huge oaks were turning to gold and crimson, the grass of the lawn was still a lush, deep green, and there were even patches of vivid red and yellow in a few late-blooming roses.

'How very considerate you are, Mrs Jeffries,' the inspector said. 'And you're right, of course. Murder cases always take so very much out of me. But I think this one might be different. I think we'll be able to ascertain the identity of the victim very, very soon.'

'I'm certain of it, sir.'

'Well, as I said, we've had a spot of luck in tracing that betrothal ring. Naturally, we started the inquiries on Bond Street. That's only reasonable, of course, considering that that is where the greatest number of jewellers are concentrated. But wouldn't you know it, the very first place Barnes tried told him that the piece had been made at Broghan's.'

'I wonder how they knew.'

'Something to do with the technique or the style or, oh, I can't remember exactly how they knew, but they did. When we got to Broghan's, the proprietor recognized the piece straight away. One of his goldsmiths had made it, and even better, he'd only sold the one.' He leaned back and beamed at her. 'And you'll never guess who he sold it to.'

'Oh, do tell, Inspector.'

'A gentleman named Emery Clements.'

Mrs Jeffries forced her expression to remain blank. As far as the inspector was concerned, she'd never heard of Emery Clements. 'I see. I presume now, that since you know who purchased the ring, you'll ask him for whom he purchased it. Correct?'

'Correct,' he confirmed. 'More importantly, we've found another very interesting connection between Mr Clements and the victim.' Witherspoon smiled smugly. 'The gentleman is also one of the major shareholders in Wildwoods Property Company.'

'Oh, don't tell me, let me guess. Wildwoods is the property company that owned the houses on Magpie Lane.'

'Right you are. Well, I'm naturally going to call around and have a chat with him as soon as possible.'

Mrs Jeffries rose to her feet as she saw Mrs Goodge waddling towards them with a crowded tea tray. 'Excuse me, sir,' she said apologetically as she rushed towards the cook. 'But I'd best take that tray from Mrs Goodge. Her rheumatism's been acting up again, and that tray looks heavy.'

'Do you want me to tell the others about Andrew Lutterbank?' Mrs Goodge whispered as she handed the tray to Mrs Jeffries.

'That's a good idea. We might not have much time this evening.' She hurried back to the inspector and set the tray on the table.

'Now, as you were saying, sir.' She poured him a cup of tea.

'Saying?' Witherspoon looked at her blankly. He'd become so engrossed in watching the sparrows chasing off an invading group of starlings that he'd forgotten what he'd just said.

'About having a chat with Mr Clements.' Mrs Jeffries finished pouring her own cup and sat down. She was rather full of tea at the moment, so she put her cup aside and gazed enquiringly at the inspector. 'You said you were going to speak with him as soon as possible.'

'Oh, yes.' Witherspoon reached for a ham sandwich. 'Unfortunately, he's out of London at the moment, but his clerk told Constable Barnes he's due back tomorrow. I'll see him then.'

Mrs Jeffries wondered where Emery Clements was and precisely what, if any, connection he had to the

dead girl. She also found it suspicious that he was conveniently out of town.

'Don't you find that rather . . . odd?' she asked.

'In what way?' Witherspoon popped a huge bite into
his mouth and chewed hungrily.

'I don't know,' she replied hesitantly, hoping he'd
catch her meaning. 'But isn't it rather strange that only
yesterday the story of finding the body was in the
papers, and today you can't find the most important
link to the girl?'

Most important link? Witherspoon frowned uncertainly. 'I'm not sure I understand what you mean.'

'The ring, sir. Wasn't it mentioned in the papers?'
Mrs Jeffries wished she'd taken the time to read them
herself this morning.

'Oh, that.' Witherspoon smiled. 'We were very
cautious in what we said to the press. There was no
mention of a betrothal ring. So even if Mr Clements
had given the deceased the ring, he'd have no way of
knowing she was the murder victim.'

He would if he killed her and buried her body in
Magpie Lane, Mrs Jeffries thought. As much as she
liked and admired her employer, there were moments
when his naïveté was annoying. Her dear late husband always used to say that when one found a murder
victim, the most likely place to look for the killer was
among the nearest and dearest. 'But the papers did say
where the body was found,' she ventured cautiously.
'And surely the name of the road should have meant
something to Mr Clements. I'm rather surprised he
didn't get in touch with the police himself.'

'But why should he?' Witherspoon reached for a bun.

'Wildwoods is a huge company. They own property all over the south of England. Magpie Lane probably meant nothing to him.'

'Yes, I'm sure you're right,' she replied. She wondered if she should tell him that that particular road did mean something to Emery Clements. But if she told him about the party in the garden and about Emery Clements's complaining about losing the rents on the abandoned houses, she'd have to tell him about their involvement in finding the missing Mary Sparks. So far, Witherspoon only knew the girl was missing and that Luty was concerned. He didn't know she and the other servants were actively searching for the girl. She decided to say nothing. Until she and the rest of the household had more information about the girl's whereabouts, her feeling was to keep silent. Mrs Jeffries had always trusted her feelings.

'We must be very delicate in the handling of this matter,' the inspector continued. 'After all, if the victim was wearing a betrothal ring given to her by Mr Clements, then that means they were engaged.'

'But didn't you mention the girl was wearing the ring on a chain around her neck?'

'Yes. But what does that have to do with it?' Witherspoon asked quizzically.

'If they were officially engaged, sir,' she pointed out, 'the victim would probably have worn the ring on her finger.'

'Oh, dear, I forgot.'

'Not to worry, sir,' she reassured him. 'You're a man. That's the sort of detail a woman remembers. Of course, she may have been wearing the ring around her neck because it was a bit too large and she didn't want to lose it. But generally, if that were the case, when the man presented it to her, he'd have noticed it didn't fit and taken it back to the jeweller for proper sizing right away.'

'Really?' Witherspoon said. He wished he'd thought of that possibility.

'Or perhaps,' Mrs Jeffries said softly, 'she had the ring around her neck because she didn't want her engagement made public.'

'Goodness, you mean people do such things?' The inspector looked thoroughly shocked. 'But why would someone get engaged and then not want anyone else to know about it?'

'For a good many reasons, sir. Parental disapproval. An inheritance, a prior engagement. Oh yes, indeed, there could be dozens of reasons why a couple would become engaged and then want it kept secret.' Satisfied that she'd made her point and that the inspector would ask Mr Clements the right questions, she broke off and smiled cheerfully.

Witherspoon stared at her dolefully. 'There are moments, Mrs Jeffries,' he said slowly, 'when I wonder if it wouldn't be a good idea to have female police officers. There are simply so many details in this world that a man just doesn't understand.'

Wiggins helped himself to another cup of cocoa. 'Garrett McGraw's safe at 'ome,' he said defensively, 'and I don't think he'll be goin' anywhere in this weather.'

A hard rain beat steadily against the kitchen windows. Betsy glanced anxiously at the door. 'Don't you think Smythe should be 'ere by now?'

'Stop worrying, Betsy,' Mrs Jeffries said soothingly. 'I'm sure he'll be along any minute.' She turned her attention back to Wiggins. 'No one is suggesting you spend the night watching the house,' she explained gently. 'We're not criticizing your decision to come home. After all, it is very late and it's pouring with rain. Betsy merely asked if Garrett did anything suspicious on his way home this evening.'

'I weren't havin' a go at you,' Betsy said. 'I only asked ya if you left the boy's street before or after the rain started.'

'After, of course. I knows me duty. I wouldn't 'ave left if'n I thought the boy was daft enough to be goin' out, and he didn't do nothing suspicious neither.' Wiggins shook his head. 'Today was the same as yesterday. The boy went straight 'ome and stayed there. No one come out but one of the little 'uns.'

'You mean Garrett's younger brother?' Mrs Goodge asked.

'That's right,' Wiggins said. 'And he did the same thing he done yesterday, scarpered off to play.'

'Obviously, we'll have to do a bit more than just keep an eye on Garrett McGraw,' Mrs Jeffries said thoughtfully.

Wiggins brightened appreciably. 'Does that mean I don't 'ave to spend every minute keepin' an eye on 'im? I can tell you, it's downright dull, and I'm gettin' awful tired of 'idin' in those bushes too. I don't care 'ow fancy that garden in Knightsbridge is, them bushes got the same bugs and briars as any other place. I almost got set on by that awful bulldog of Major Parkinson's. He's a real vicious brute, and he woulda 'ad me if'n I 'adn't jumped the fence.' He looked down in despair at his torn trousers.

'Yes, I'm sure your experience was dreadful,' Mrs Jeffries said quickly. 'You won't have to spend all of your time watching Garrett McGraw.' They'd heard the bulldog story several times already. She didn't relish listening to it again. She glanced at the clock. 'Perhaps tomorrow, I'll try my luck with the boy. Gracious, it is getting late. We can't wait any longer for Smythe.'

They'd deliberately waited until after Inspector Witherspoon had gone to bed before convening around the kitchen table to compare notes. Smythe was the only one who wasn't here, but Mrs Jeffries knew from experience that the coachman could take care of himself, so she wasn't too concerned. They'd have to start without him.

Mrs Goodge had already told Wiggins and Betsy the gossip she'd heard about Andrew Lutterbank.

'Betsy.' Mrs Jeffries said, 'would you like to tell us what you've found out today?'

'I don't know, Mrs Jeffries.' Betsy gave the back door another worried glance. 'It don't feel right startin' without Smythe.'

'Your feelings are very understandable, but this isn't the first time we've had a meeting without him.' Considering the rivalry between the coachman and the maid, Betsy's insistence was rather surprising. But perhaps not, Mrs Jeffries thought, as she studied the girl. They all shared a sense of camaraderie and fair play in their little adventures. Yet as she saw the girl flick another anxious glance at the back door, another idea struck her.

Betsy's china-blue eyes had gone to the door half a dozen times in the last few minutes. She was genuinely worried about the coachman. No. It couldn't be, Mrs Jeffries told herself. Smythe and Betsy were as different as chalk and cheese. Surely this lovely, fair-haired girl hadn't developed an infatuation for their big, almost brutal-looking coachman. She was instantly ashamed of herself for thinking of Smythe in those terms. He might be large and cursed with prominent features and a swarthy countenance, but he was one of nature's true gentlemen. Mrs Jeffries couldn't think of anyone she'd rather have by her side when trouble came.

She was being silly. Of course Betsy and Smythe weren't interested in each other – why, what an odd idea. The maid was merely a bit jittery because the wind was howling and the night was black as sin.

'Remember when we were investigaing the Slocum murder,' Mrs Jeffries reminded her gently. 'Smythe disappeared for several days. When he finally appeared, he was perfectly all right and downright full of himself to boot.'

'True,' Betsy agreed. 'He was right proud of himself that time, wasn't he?'

''E 'ad reason to be,' Wiggins said in defence of his friend. ''E did find out a lot about old Slocum's nephew being a thief.'

'Yes, yes, of course he did,' Mrs Jeffries said impatiently. 'Now, it's getting very late, and we really must get on with the business at hand.'

Betsy nodded reluctantly. 'All right, then. I did like you said and I went back to the shop. 'Ad a bit of luck there too. The manager was busy in the back, so I got a chance to get Ellen Wickes a talkin'.' She grinned. 'Ellen was right jealous of Cassie Yates. She told me that Cassie was always braggin' about the men 'angin' round and wantin' to marry her. 'Course, Ellen claims at first she didn't believe her. Thought Cassie were tellin' tales and makin' up stories to make 'erself look important.'

'What happened to change her mind?' Mrs Goodge asked.

'The men started comin' round the shop. That changed Ellen's tune fast enough.' Betsy leaned forward on her elbows. 'Three of 'em.'

'Three!' Wiggins looked positively scandalized. 'That's disgustin'.'

The footman was a hopeless romantic. Mrs Jeffries made a mental note to give him back the love poem she'd found lying on the pantry table this afternoon. Perhaps she'd gently encourage him to try another method of expressing his feelings about the housemaid from up the road. 'Your cheeks as round as the moon in June,' might be a bit offensive. Sarah Trippet could feel he was saying she had a fat face.

Betsy shrugged. 'Disgustin' or not, that's what Ellen told me. And she said all three of the men were real sweet on Cassie.'

Mrs Jeffries asked, 'Did she say how she knew that?'

'Of course she did. I tell you, Mrs Jeffries, the girl was dishin' out the dirt on Cassie Yates faster than a dog digs a bone. She said she seen the first bloke, a great big tall blond feller, call for Cassie in a fancy carriage at least twice. Cassie claimed 'e was takin' her to one of them posh restaurants over on the Strand both times.' Betsy stroked her chin. 'Ellen saw the second man a couple of days after the first one took Cassie out to supper. He was a heavyset bloke, with dark hair and chin whiskers. Cassie claims he took her to the opera and then to supper afterwards. Ellen said he looked like a real gent – 'ad on expensive clothes and all.'

'And the third man?' Mrs Jeffries prompted. Betsy did tend to get carried away.

'Now, that's the interestin' one – Cassie was right cagey about the third bloke,' Betsy said meaningfully. 'She didn't say much about him to Ellen.'

Mrs Jeffries looked disappointed. 'Oh, dear. So you don't know much about him, then?'

Betsy grinned. 'I knows plenty about 'im. Cassie wouldn't talk much about the feller, but that didn't stop Ellen from doin' a bit of snooping. Seems he only called around the shop twice. Both times on foot too. When Cassie wouldn't say much, Ellen got curious. So the second time he come around, Ellen claimed she just 'appened to be leavin' just after them. She claims she just 'appened to follow them up the street. They stopped at a park and the man pulls her behind a tree. Ellen says she saw him give Cassie something. Something small.'

Mrs Goodge snorted. 'Ellen Wickes saw all this, did she?'

Betsy shrugged. 'She says she just happened to catch it out of the corner of her eye, but I reckon she was following them and spyin' on them.'

'Did Ellen ask Cassie about him?' Mrs Jeffries asked. She was glad to hear Betsy restoring her hs to their proper place. She wished she could get the girl to concentrate as easily on the final g of her words, but she didn't like to correct her in front of the others, and in all fairness, except when she was terribly excited, Betsy was very careful with her pronunciation.

'No. Ellen were dyin' to know who the man was, but she told me she wouldn't lower herself to ask. Besides, Cassie talked free enough about her men. Ellen figured it were just a matter of time before she said somethin'.'

'I don't suppose Ellen was able to give you any names?'

'No. But one of the other maids at the Lutterbanks' house did,' Betsy said proudly. 'After I finished talkin' to Ellen, I went to Knightsbridge. Honestly, Mrs Jeffries, it was too easy. I 'adn't been there more than three minutes when one of the parlourmaids come out and hotfoots it down the street. She was takin' a note to the butcher, and I caught her when she come out of the shop. She 'ad even more to say about Cassie than Ellen did.'

'‘Ow do ya get them to talk so fast?' Wiggins asked curiously.

'Oh, that's easy,' Betsy explained loftily. 'I just start askin' questions. When they ask me why I'm askin', I tell 'em that Cassie Yates told a pack of lies about me and I lost me position because of it. I tell them I want to get a bit of me own back.'

The footman gazed at her in open admiration. 'Cor, that's a good 'un. I'll have to try that sometime meself.'

'You've got to play your story a bit by ear,' Betsy explained earnestly, 'dependin' on who you're tryin' to get information on, but I figured that with someone like Cassie Yates . . .'

'Speaking of which,' Mrs Jeffries interrupted firmly, 'could we please stop digressing and get back to the matter at hand? I believe Betsy was going to give us the names of the men who'd been seen with Cassie.'

'Malcolm Farnsworth and Emery Clements,' Betsy stated hurriedly. She blushed and leaned back in the chair. 'Accordin' to the parlourmaid, Cassie was seein' both of them.'

Mrs Goodge frowned heavily. 'What about the third one, then?'

'She didn't know his name. But she knew there was someone else. She seen her with him. Cassie weren't one to keep conquests to 'erself.'

Emery Clements was certainly a familiar name, Mrs Jeffries thought. For that matter, so was the name Malcolm. 'Malcolm Farnsworth,' she said thoughtfully. 'I wonder if that's Antonia Everdene's fiancé. I know his Christian name is Malcolm.'

Betsy gaped at her. 'How'd you find that out?'

'I went to the Everdene house today,' Mrs Jeffries admitted. 'I'll tell you all about it in a minute. First, though, I want to hear the rest of what you've found out. Did you question the parlourmaid about Mary Sparks?'

'Didn't have much luck there . . .' Betsy paused. 'But you know, it's right strange. When I asked Abby, that's the parlourmaid, if there'd been any stealin' goin' on, the girl said there hadn't. Don't you think if an expensive brooch was stolen, she'd a known about it?'

Mrs Jeffries frowned. 'Yes, one would think so.'

'I think so too. But even when I were hintin' that maybe that's why Mary Sparks left the Lutterbanks,

Abby just shook her head and said no. Claimed Mary just up and left one day. There weren't no fuss made about a stolen brooch or anything else. Abby were right surprised too. She thought Mary and Mark McGraw had an understandin' – Mary had been sayin' she was goin' to keep on workin' for the Lutterbanks until Mark come home.'

Mrs Jeffries drew a sharp breath. 'So the household didn't know about the alleged theft.'

'Not a word. And, if you ask me, it's downright impossible,' Betsy said flatly. 'There in't a 'ouse in London that can keep that kind of gossip out of the servants' 'all. Oh, I did think to ask her what Mary was wearin' the day she left.'

'What's that got to do with anythin'?' Wiggins asked.

Betsy ignored him. 'She 'ad on her blue dress and a pair of dark shoes. But they wasn't new shoes. I asked Abby about that too. She said Mary was still wearin' a pair of old brown ones.'

Mrs Jeffries beamed in approval. 'Very good, Betsy. Now, as we've already heard what Mrs Goodge and Wiggins learned today, it's my turn.'

Just then, they heard the screech of the hinges as the back door opened and Smythe stepped inside. He was soaked. Water dripped from his coat onto the floor, his shoes squeaked with every step, and his dark hair was plastered flat against his skin.

Betsy leapt to her feet. 'You're soaked, man. Get that wet coat off before you catch yer death.' She dashed behind him and tugged at the wet garment.

'Stop yer fussin',' he said with a lazy grin. 'A bit of water never hurt anyone. I see ya started without me.'

While he was stripping off his coat and drying off before the stove, Mrs Jeffries told him everything the others had discovered that day.

'I was just starting to tell everyone what I'd learned today when you came in,' she finished. 'So I may as well continue. As I said before. I went to the Everdene house today, and I must say, I think Antonia Everdene knows something about Mary Sparks's disappearance.'

'I should bloomin' well 'ope so,' Smythe muttered as he settled gratefully into a chair.

Mrs Jeffries looked at him sharply. 'Why?'

'You'd best finish first,' he said sombrely. 'When you 'ear what I've found out, it'll become clear enough.'

She stared at him for a moment and then went ahead and told them everything. Naturally, she gave them every little detail of the visit. 'All right, Smythe,' she commanded softly as soon as she finished with her story. 'It's your turn now.'

He took his time answering, his big, dark eyes staring blankly into space for a few moments. 'I've spent most of today lookin' for the livery that hired the carriage that come to take away Cassie Yates's belongin's,' he finally said. He glanced at the housekeeper. 'It weren't Howards. It were Steptons over near the Wandsworth Bridge. One of the blokes there remembers a toff comin' in on September the eleventh and hirin' the carriage, but he weren't the one that did the drivin', and he wouldn't sneak a peek at the logbook for me. He did give me the name of the feller that drove the carriage that day, but the man's gone to Bristol to visit his relations and in't due back for a few days.'

'So we'll have to wait until he comes back to find out

just who it was that took away Cassie Yates's belongings,' Mrs Jeffries said. Her apprehension mounted. Smythe was certainly taking a long time to get to the point. If it had been Mrs Goodge talking, she'd have thought nothing of it, but he never beat around the bush.

'Right.' Smythe began drumming his fingers against the top of the table.

Mrs Jeffries cleared her throat, and when Smythe looked up at her, she gave him a long, level stare. 'What else did you learn today?' she asked quietly.

His mouth flattened into a grim line. 'I found the driver that picked Mary Sparks up the night she left Knightsbridge.'

'Where'd he take her?' Betsy asked.

'This was the day after she'd supposedly gone to the Everdene house, right?' Mrs Goodge said. Her eyes were narrowed in concentration.

'Yeah. It took me a long time to track the bloke, I chased him over 'alf of London today . . .'

'Smythe,' Mrs Jeffries interrupted. 'Please tell us what you've learned.'

He took a deep breath, and his big body slumped against the back of the chair. 'The driver picked Mary up just after it got dark. But you're not goin' to like where he took 'er.' He paused and rubbed one hand over his face. 'He drove her to Magpie Lane.'

There was a horrid, stunned silence. Mrs Jeffries was the first to find her voice. 'But Luty Belle was sure the body wasn't Mary . . .'

'Cor, I know that,' Smythe exclaimed. 'But she must've been wrong.'

Wiggins's chubby round face twisted into a scowl. 'I don't understand what you're all on about. Why's everyone gettin' in such a state?'

'Because if'n he took Mary to Magpie Lane that night,' Mrs Goodge explained irritably, 'no matter what Luty Belle Crookshank says, the dead girl is probably Mary Sparks.'

'But Mary had small feet,' Wiggins protested.

'That don't mean nuthin',' Betsy interjected. 'If'n you're poor and you come across a brand new pair of shoes, you go ahead and grab 'em.'

'How could she keep 'em on her feet?' he argued. 'If'n they's too big, they'd have come off.'

'They were high-button shoes,' Mrs Jeffries said quickly. 'Mary could have stuffed the toes with newspapers.'

'I don't believe it,' Wiggins insisted.

Mrs Jeffries wished she didn't have to believe it either. No wonder Smythe wasn't crowing like the cock of the walk tonight. He'd probably dreaded having to share this particular bit of news. Luty Belle was going to be dreadfully upset.

'Wiggins,' Mrs Jeffries said gently. 'None of us want to believe it. But the facts do speak for themselves. Mary has been missing for two months. A body that's been dead for approximately the same amount of time has been found in Magpie Lane. If Smythe's information is correct, and we've no reason to think it isn't, the last time anyone saw Mary alive was the night she was taken to Magpie Lane.'

CHAPTER SIX

Inspector Witherspoon knew it wasn't going be a good day. He glanced at the clerk working in the corner of the outer office of Wildwoods and stifled a sigh. Outside the narrow windows the sky loomed cloudy and ominous. He could hear the clatter of the omnibuses and the clip-clop of horses' hooves blending with the raucous cries of the street vendors.

He frowned at the closed door of Emery Clements's office and wished the man would hurry up so he could get this uncomfortable interview over. Witherspoon hated asking questions of a personal nature. He much preferred the nice, easy straightforward inquiries such as what is your name, what is your address and where were you at such and such a time. Yet now he had to go into that office and ask Mr Clements about a betrothal ring and possibly even a fiancée. Goodness, he thought, this could turn out to be a crime of passion. The idea made Witherspoon shudder. No, he decided, it definitely wasn't going to be a good day. But much as he dreaded the coming interview, he still found himself hoping that Emery Clements could give them some useful information. The Chief Inspector was beginning to make pointed remarks. So far they hadn't identified the victim, located the murder weapon or found any witnesses. None of his police constables were getting anywhere with their door-to-door inquiries around Magpie Lane, nor had they had any success in locating the shop that had sold the victim her shoes. If he didn't find something useful soon, he simply wouldn't know what to do next. Even his household had been glum and morose this morning.

The door opened, and a thin-faced clerk stuck his head out. 'Inspector Witherspoon, Mr Clements can see you now.'

Witherspoon straightened his spine and trailed the clerk into the inner office. Constable Barnes, who'd been hovering by the front door, followed.

A tall, heavyset gentleman dressed in a beautifully tailored black frock coat, grey waistcoat and white shirt, with a narrow tie under a wing-tipped collar, rose from behind a mahogany desk. He had brown hair, a neat beard topped with a handlebar moustache and a florid complexion.

'Good morning, Inspector. I'm Emery Clements. My clerk says you'd like to talk to me. I must say I'm a bit mystified,' he began, not bothering to hide his irritation at the interruption. 'I can't imagine what interest the police could possibly have in me.'

'Good morning, sir,' Witherspoon replied. 'I'm Inspector Gerald Witherspoon and this is Constable Barnes.'

Clements acknowledged the constable with a barely perceptible nod and then turned his attention back to Inspector Witherspoon.

'Please sit down.' Clements motioned to the one chair in front of the desk. The inspector sat. 'Now, sir, why don't you tell me what this is all about?'

'I understand, Mr Clements, that you've an account at Broghan's on Holland Park Road. Is that correct?' Witherspoon tried to infuse his voice with authority. He hadn't liked the way his constable had been treated. Surely it wouldn't have been too much trouble to find a chair for Barnes as well.

Clements arched one bushy eyebrow. 'That's correct, but I can't see why that's any concern of Scotland Yard.'

'I assure you, sir, it is our concern.' The inspector reached into his pocket, drew out a small cloth bag, opened it, lifted out the betrothal ring and laid it on the top of the desk. 'The manager at Broghan's said this ring was charged to your account. That was on September the ninth. Would you mind telling us the name of the lady you gave it to? It is, as you can see, a betrothal ring.'

For a moment, Clements stared at the ring. When he lifted his chin and gazed at the inspector, he looked genuinely puzzled. 'There's obviously been some sort of a mistake here. I've no idea what you're talking about. I've never seen this ring in my life.'

Witherspoon's heart sank. The Chief Inspector wasn't going to be pleased. 'But it was charged to your account. The manager was quite sure about that.'

'Yes, well, I'll have to have a word with the manager about his shoddy record-keeping practices, won't I? I certainly would remember if I purchased something like this.' He tapped his finger at the ring. 'An engagement is generally a rather important event in one's life, Inspector. I assure you, it isn't the sort of occasion I'd forget.'

'So you can tell us nothing about it?' Witherspoon asked.

'I'm afraid not. Now, if you'll excuse me, I've a rather busy day planned . . .' Clements broke off and then suddenly smiled. 'Wait a moment. Now I know what happened. Of course, how stupid of me not to remember.'

'Remember what?' Witherspoon glanced at Barnes to make sure he was taking notes. He was.

'Inspector, you're quite right, that ring was charged to my account.' Clements gave a hearty laugh. 'But I wasn't the one who actually purchased it. I allowed a friend of mine who'd just become engaged to a lovely lady to use my account. He was in a, shall we say, somewhat embarrassing financial position.'

The inspector thought it odd that one could forget allowing a friend to use one's account at a very expensive jeweller's. He wondered if there were anything else Emery Clements had forgotten. Perhaps the man had forgotten any number of important facts. 'What's this friend's name?' Witherspoon asked.

Clements's smile disappeared. 'Would you mind telling me what this is all about? I've no wish to appear uncooperative, but really, sir, you have started asking what I consider most impertinent questions. Who I allow to use my accounts is my concern and my concern only.'

Witherspoon felt a blush creep up his cheeks. By all rights, Mr Clements did deserve an explanation.

Generally, he always told people straight off why he'd come to see them, but with this particular gentleman, he'd had a strong feeling that keeping silent would net some results. He'd been hoping for some sort of reaction when he produced the ring, yet all he'd seen was genuine puzzlement. Drat.

'We've no wish to intrude upon your privacy, Mr Clements,' Witherspoon explained. 'But unfortunately, we've no choice in this case. We must find out who owned this ring. It was found on the body of a murdered woman.'

Clements jerked back as if he'd been shot. 'Good Lord. Murder? I take it this isn't a joke.' His brows drew together into one line across his face. 'I do believe, sir, you should have informed me you were investigating a murder before I began answering any of your questions.'

'Why?' the inspector asked honestly, briefly wondering if there'd been some new judges' rules issued lately that he'd missed.

'Why?' Clements was incredulous. 'Why, you ask. My dear sir, I'd no idea when you popped in here asking questions that you were investigating a murder.'

'Would you have answered differently if you had known?' Witherspoon asked. He wondered why the man was making such a fuss. He either knew something about the ring or he didn't. But perhaps, he thought craftily, Mr Clements knew something after all. Something he didn't want the police to know.

'Of course not.' Clements clamped his mouth shut and took a deep breath. 'I'm not sure but that I shouldn't have my solicitor present before I answer any more questions.'

'That is your right,' Witherspoon answered. He watched him carefully for a few seconds, looking for signs of distress or guilt. But the man didn't look in the least guilty. He merely appeared annoyed. But why should he be angry if he hadn't bought the wretched ring? Oh, dear. The inspector felt another one of those nasty headaches coming on. He thought longingly of his former job in the records room. Then he remembered his duty and the poor young woman who'd had her life so brutally ended. He also remembered where her body had been found. Witherspoon stopped worrying about whether or not he was irritating Emery Clements. There were a few more questions that needed to be answered here. 'We'll be happy to wait while you send one of your clerks for your solicitor.'

Clements gazed at Witherspoon uncertainly. Then he held up his hand. 'Actually, there's no need to bother him. My solicitor and I are both very busy men. Frankly, I don't want to take any more time on this matter than is absolutely necessary. I've no idea how that ring ended up on the hand of a murdered woman, but I can assure you, it's nothing to do with me or the gentleman I allowed to use my account.'

'Good. Then we'll carry on, shall we?' The inspector smiled politely.

Clements nodded stiffly. He took a long, deep breath and asked, 'Who was the victim?'

'We're not sure,' Witherspoon replied.

'You're not sure?' Clements repeated. 'What does that mean?'

'It means, sir, that when the body was found, it was decomposed to the point where it was impossible to make any identification whatsoever.' He watched Clements's face go pale.

'My God.' Clements looked down at his desk. 'Decomposed,' he mumbled. 'How dreadful. How awful.'

The inspector noticed that the man's hands, which had been lying flat on the desk, were now balled into tight fists. The inspector cleared his throat. 'I know this is rather shocking news,' he said softly, 'but you can see why it's rather important we trace the ring.'

'Yes, yes. Of course I can.' Clements took another deep breath and seemed to get ahold of himself. 'I'm afraid what I've got to tell you won't be of much use.'

'Why don't you let us be the judge of that? We'd still like that name.'

Clements ignored him and instead asked a question of his own. 'Could you tell me, when was this unfortunate woman murdered?'

Witherspoon saw no reason not to answer. 'Approximately two months ago.'

Clements's mouth turned down in disgust. 'Two months ago? That doesn't sound very nice.'

'Yes, well, that's why the victim was decomposed, you see. The murderer buried her in a cellar, and the body was only found two days ago,' Witherspoon explained.

'Then obviously, there has been a mistake. I've seen the young woman my friend purchased the betrothal ring for, and I can assure you, that as of yesterday she was alive and well. So quite obviously, there's been some sort of muddle in the identification of the ring.'

Witherspoon knew there hadn't been any mistakes. The jeweller who'd made the ring had been positive. But he saw no reason to share that information with Emery Clements. 'May I please have their names?' he asked patiently.

'Malcolm Farnsworth is the person I allowed to use my account,' Clements admitted grudgingly. 'He's engaged to a Miss Antonia Everdene.'

'The engagement was recent?' The inspector decided to ask any question that popped into his head. It seemed as good a way as any to get the man talking . . .

'No,' Clements answered quickly. 'They became engaged in September. But I've already told you. There's obviously been a terrible mistake. Malcolm's fiancée is alive and well. I've told you, I saw the lady myself.'

Witherspoon regarded him thoughtfully. 'I understand you own the property on Magpie Lane.'

'My company does. Why?' His eyes narrowed suspiciously. 'What's that got to do with it?'

'The body was found buried in the cellar of one of those houses. Your own clerk has confirmed the houses were sitting empty for several months without tenants before they were demolished.' Witherspoon leaned forward. 'Tell me, sir, have you any idea what that young woman was doing wearing a ring bought on your account and in one of the properties your company owns?'

'Certainly not,' Clements exclaimed, 'and I must

116

say, I don't like your attitude or the implications of your questions.'

Witherspoon caught himself. 'My question wasn't meant to imply anything. I was merely wondering if perhaps you knew of any reason a young woman would ensconce herself in an abandoned house.'

'How should I know?' Clements leaned on his elbows and twined his fingers together. 'As you said, those houses had been sitting empty for a long time. There was a dispute between the local authority and the underground rail builders. The land was originally cleared for the purpose of widening the road. But there was some kind of argument, and at the last minute everything changed and it was decided to build the underground.'

'I see,' Witherspoon said slowly. He gazed steadily at Emery Clements. 'You know, sir, that's how the body was found. She was buried in the cellar. The workers digging the exploratory trench found her.'

Clements closed his eyes briefly. Witherspoon began to revise his first impression of the man. He actually seemed genuinely moved by this poor woman's murder. Perhaps Mr Clements hadn't invited Constable Barnes to sit down because he didn't think police constables were supposed to be seated while they took notes.

'How was she killed?' Clements asked softly.

As that information had already been ferreted out by the press, the inspector could see no reason not to answer. 'She was stabbed.'

'Appalling.'

'Very.' The inspector got to his feet. 'Could you

please give me Malcolm Farnsworth's address? Naturally, we'll need to talk to him.'

'He lives with me,' Clements replied. 'We've been friends since our school days together. When he came to London a few years ago, I invited him to stay with my mother and me.' He started to write the address on a piece of paper.

'We have your address,' Witherspoon told him. 'Is Mr Farnsworth at home now?'

'I've no idea.'

Witherspoon smiled slightly. 'Can you tell us where he works?'

'Mr Farnsworth has a private income,' Clements said. 'His job is managing his investments. Naturally, he works at home. If he isn't there, you can try his club.'

'And which club would that be, sir?' Constable Barnes interjected softly.

Clements appeared to be surprised that the constable could speak. 'Picketts. It's near Regent's Park.'

'We know where it is, sir,' Witherspoon said quickly.

They left the office shortly after that. Barnes waited till they'd turned the corner onto Wellington Street before he began asking questions. 'What did you think of him, sir?' he asked with a half-smile.

'I'm not sure, Barnes,' Witherspoon replied. He frowned at the heavy traffic and then turned and walked towards Waterloo Bridge and the river. A tram on its way to Temple Station momentarily obscured his view of the river. Sighing, he said, 'Not a likable fellow, but he did seem genuinely distressed by the murder. Still, I don't suppose the man has any reason to lie to us . . .'

'He does if he's the killer,' Barnes muttered. He was still smarting over having to stand and take notes. 'And his acting all concerned about the poor girl bein' done in and buried in that cellar could be an act.'

'Hmmm. Well, yes, but we've no evidence he is the killer, have we? But still, there's something decidedly peculiar about his story,' Witherspoon said.

'Like what, sir?'

'I didn't like the way he hedged over giving us those names.

Surely, when a man hears there's been a murder committed, he immediately wants to tell the police everything he knows.' Witherspoon increased his pace. 'But that wasn't how Mr Clements reacted at all. Even after he knew why we were there, he didn't want to tell us who had used his account at Broghan's to buy that ring.'

'And then, of course, there's the body bein' found on his property,' Barnes added.

'Right, Constable. I don't like it. I don't like it at all.' Witherspoon jabbed his finger in the air for emphasis. 'There's more to this case than meets the eye, I can tell you that.'

'Where to now, sir?' Barnes was practically having to run to keep up with the inspector.

'To the tramway,' the inspector replied. 'I want to stop in at the Yard and go over those workmen's statements before we pay a call on Mr Malcolm Farnsworth.'

Mrs Jeffries, Betsy, Smythe and Mrs Goodge were half-heartedly tending to their chores. Betsy was polishing the silver, Mrs Goodge was leafing through her recipe book, Smythe was filling the coal bins and Mrs Jeffries was counting sheets.

After they'd heard Smythe's depressing news of the night before, the only one who'd faced the day with any enthusiasm was Wiggins.

At breakfast, he'd bounced into the room and announced he was going back to Knightsbridge for 'another go at Garrett McGraw'. No matter how they all protested it was useless, he wouldn't be deterred. Mrs Jeffries wasn't sure what to make of such behaviour. But the boy was so convinced that Mary was still alive, she didn't have the heart to try and stop him. Truth to tell, she wasn't sure she wanted to either. He'd soon enough come to the same conclusion the rest of them had arrived at last night.

Mary was dead.

Mrs Jeffries shoved the linen basket into the corner and then stood there staring at the wall. Her conscience bothered her. She should have gone to Luty Belle's as soon as she got up that morning, but she'd deliberately been putting it off. Well, she told herself, stop dithering and get to it. The sooner she got this uncomfortable duty over with, the better.

The gloom of the overcast day matched Mrs Jeffries's mood as she walked with Luty Belle in the communal gardens behind the row of tall townhouses. The elderly woman was not taking the news very well. She didn't, in fact, appear to have heard a word Mrs Jeffries had said.

'I tell you, that corpse weren't Mary Sparks.' Luty shook her head vehemently. 'I knows it. I kin feel it.'

'Now, Luty,' Mrs Jeffries said gently. 'None of us

want to believe that Mary is dead, but the facts speak for themselves.' She stopped by the gate and pointed towards the street beyond. 'Mary left the gardens from right here. She walked out of that gate, got in a hansom and was taken to Magpie Lane. She hasn't been seen or heard from since.'

'That don't mean she's dead,' Luty said stubbornly.

'The body of a young woman wearing Mary's clothes was found buried in the cellar of a house in Magpie Lane,' Mrs Jeffries continued doggedly. 'As dreadfully awful as it is, we've got to face facts.'

'An' the one fact you seem to be forgettin', missy, is that them shoes on that body weren't Mary's.' Luty banged her cane against the ground for emphasis.

Mrs Jeffries gazed helplessly at the stubborn old woman and wondered how to convince her of the truth. 'But as Betsy pointed out,' she began, 'Mary had very little money. Perhaps she found those shoes, and they were in such good condition, she decided to wear them despite the fact they were too large.'

'Horse patties,' Luty cried. 'Mary wouldn't have happened to find a pair of brand-new shoes, and I know fer a fact she wouldna wasted what little money she had buyin' 'em. Besides, she didn't steal that danged brooch, and you said it were pinned to the dress when they found her.'

'I'm not accusing her of theft,' Mrs Jeffries explained. 'But there's another solution to that particular mystery.'

Luty cocked her head to one side. 'An jus' what's that?'

'The murderer could have pinned that brooch on Mary's dress after she was killed.'

121

'She's alive,' Luty insisted stubbornly. 'I know it. I kin feel it.'

Mrs Jeffries took her arm and led her to one of the wooden benches under an elm tree. When they were sitting, she said, 'I know exactly how you feel. I don't want to believe the girl's dead either. But the facts speak for themselves.' She held up her hand for silence when Luty opened her mouth to protest. 'Furthermore, you're not doing Mary any good by letting her murderer get away with this foul deed.'

'But I ain't doin' that!'

'Yes, you are,' Mrs Jeffries said firmly. 'Every minute we waste our time and energy looking for the girl, in the mistaken belief that she is alive, is one more minute for the killer to cover his tracks. If we're not careful, if we don't start concentrating on who actually took her life, he'll get away with it.' She paused and gave Luty a long, hard stare. 'Is that what you want?'

Luty glared at her for a few seconds and then she quickly turned away. Her thin shoulders slumped as she gazed at a pile of fallen leaves. 'No,' she whispered in a trembling voice. 'If'n Mary is dead, I want the one that did it to hang.'

They sat in silence for a few moments before Luty straightened and turned to Mrs Jeffries. 'All right, we'll have it yur way. Mary's dead. I don't like it, but I never was one to hide my head in a hole when the truth of the matter was smacking me in the face.'

'I know it's hard, Luty. But the only thing we can do for the girl now is to find her killer.'

'What do you want me to do?' Luty asked, staring at Mrs Jeffries shrewdly.

'I want you to tell Inspector Witherspoon everything you know.' She reached over and patted the wrinkled hand that held the top of the cane in a death grip.

'What good'll that do?' Luty snorted.

'Well, for one thing, it will put him on the right track. Once he knows the victim is definitely Mary Sparks, he can start questioning everyone she had contact with prior to her death. We know that Mary must have been killed after she left here on the tenth. With that date as a starting point and all the other information we've managed to learn about the Everdenes, the Lutterbanks and Cassie Yates, he's bound to come up with something.'

'You reckon one of that bunch is the killer?' Luty asked softly.

'It's possible.'

'Are you and the others still goin' to be sniffin' around too? No offence meant to yur inspector, but I won't feel right if'n you all just hand everythin' over to the police.'

'Don't worry, Luty,' Mrs Jeffries assured her. 'We'll most definitely be sniffing around. Now, I think I'd better bring you up to date on our investigation. You'll need to pass this information along to the inspector.'

For the next half hour, Mrs Jeffries gave Luty every little detail. She told her about her visit to the Everdene house, Betsy's investigation of Cassie Yates, about Wiggins's perpetual watch on Garrett McGraw and about Smythe's finding the hansom driver who took Mary to Magpie Lane. Luty snorted in disgust as Mrs Jeffries related Mrs Goodge's gossip about Andrew Lutterbank and the girl he'd got pregnant. 'I remember the girl,' Luty said. 'Real sweet, used to like to talk every now and agin when she could git away from the house. Sally Comstock was her name. She used to like to do embroidery. Some of the other girls laughed at her, said she were givin' herself airs. Always embroidering her initials on everythin' she owned. Reckon they was probably jealous – she were a right purty girl.'

'You mean you knew about the scandal? Why didn't you tell us this before?'

''Cause I didn't remember until you just now reminded me.' Luty shrugged. 'And it weren't all that much of a scandal at the time. The family was purty good at hushin' everythin' up. Even I wouldna known if'n Mrs Devlin, the Lutterbank housekeeper, hadna happened to mention it . . . but that was several weeks after the family had got rid of the girl.' She shrugged. 'That scandal don't have nuthin' to do with Mary anyhows. Sally Comstock was gone before Mary started workin' for the Lutterbanks. Matter of fact, last time I even saw poor Sally was at old Angus's funeral.'

'Is there anything else you know about Andrew Lutterbank?'

'Just what I told you before. Don't reckon he's much count. The women like him fine, what with all his dandy clothes and smooth manners. But he's got a mean streak a mile wide. Holds a bad grudge too.'

'How do you know that?' Mrs Jeffries asked curiously.

'Hatchet told me. Don't let that poker face of his fool ya, the man's as nosy as a curious cat. Hears more gossip around these parts than I do.' Luty sighed. 'Come to think of it, I reckon I should have remembered all this before now, but that's what comes of gittin' old. Sometimes things slip your mind.'

'You're not old, Luty,' Mrs Jeffries assured her. 'And how does your butler know that Andrew Lutterbank holds a grudge?'

'One of the Lutterbank footmen told him. When Andrew was away at school, one of the other boys got him into some kind of trouble,' Luty explained. 'Lutterbank waited for years to get even – Hatchet didn't know all the details, but it seems Andrew managed to squeeze whoever it was that wronged him out of a real good investment deal. The footman knew about it because Andrew was braggin' to his friends about how he never forgot an enemy. He once tried to whip his coachman too, but the man was bigger than him.' Luty broke off and shook her head. 'But I don't reckon he murdered Mary. She didn't like him much, but she weren't scared of him. Besides, he ain't got no reason to have killed her.'

'None that we know of anyway,' Mrs Jeffries added. Until they knew more about the murder, she was prepared to consider anyone who'd known Mary a suspect.

Luty pursed her lips. 'How am I supposed to tell the inspector I come by all this information?' she asked. 'I knows none of you want me lettin' on that you're helpin'.'

'Oh, that's quite simple.' Mrs Jeffries smiled. 'Come by the house this evening and tell him everything I've told you. If he asks, and there is always the chance that he won't, tell him you were so concerned you hired a private inquiry agent – an American inquiry agent who has since left.'

'You don't expect he'd be dumb enough to believe that?' Luty said incredulously. 'Come on now, Hepzibah, that kind of yarn wouldn't fool a child, let alone an inspector from Scotland Yard.'

For a moment Mrs Jeffries was at a loss. 'Oh, dear, I do hope I haven't given you the wrong impression. Inspector Witherspoon isn't stupid,' she explained. 'But he is very, well, trusting. Actually, that particular trait is the reason he's so successful as a detective. People are constantly underestimating him; consequently they don't guard their tongues and they inevitably give themselves away.' It was a very thin explanation, and Mrs Jeffries knew it. From Luty's caustic expression Mrs Jeffries suspected that she knew it too.

'All right, I'll be by around eight.' Luty kicked her cane to the ground and leapt to her feet.

Mrs Jeffries hid her smile. She'd suspected that Luty didn't need a cane any more than Betsy did. She also suspected that the only reason the woman carried it was that she couldn't carry a gun in the streets of London. Luty had once confessed to her that when she and her husband had moved here after years of living in the Wild West of America, giving up her six-shooter had almost killed her. Any weapon, even a stick, was better than none. 'I think that'll work perfectly, Luty.'

Mrs Jeffries's spirits were better when she arrived back in Upper Edmonton Gardens. She took off her coat and hat and hurried down to the kitchen.

Betsy looked up from the silver serving spoon she had been slowly polishing, Mrs Goodge grunted a hello and Smythe nodded and then hunched back over his cup of tea.

'Luty took the news as well as can be expected,' she announced quickly, 'and apparently she and Wiggins are the only ones who realize we've still got a murder to solve.'

'Give us a bit o' time, Mrs Jeffries,' Betsy whined. 'We all know there's a killer out there somewhere, but it'll take a day or two to get over the upset. Even though none of us knew Mary, we'd all got right fond of 'er just listening to Luty Belle talk about the girl.'

'I'm aware of that,' Mrs Jeffries said firmly. 'But we don't have a day or two to play about.'

'Mary's not in no 'urry,' Smythe complained. 'She's been dead two months now.'

Mrs Goodge sighed. 'Rotten luck.'

Mrs Jeffries felt like shaking the lot of them. 'I know how you all feel,' she said. 'But we're not going to find Mary's murderer by sitting around here and moaning. Come on, now. Get up. There's work to be done.'

Smythe arched one heavy black brow. 'And exactly what do ya wan' us to do?'

'First of all, I want you to find that driver who came and collected Cassie Yates's belongings from the lodging house.'

'But why?' Betsy asked in confusion. 'Cassie don't have nuthin' to do with Mary's murder. She weren't the one buried in Magpie Lane.'

'I'm not sure why,' Mrs Jeffries replied honestly. 'But Ellen Wickes said that Cassie ran out of the shop and chased a young woman around the corner – all she saw was the skirt of the woman's dress, but remember, it was a dark blue dress.'

'I get it. It might 'ave been Mary that Cassie was chasin' after.' Smythe jumped to his feet. 'Is that what yur sayin'?'

'That's it exactly.'

The kitchen was suddenly filled with suppressed excitement. Betsy's eyes began to sparkle, Mrs Goodge shoved her recipe book into a drawer and Smythe dashed to the back door, eager to be off on the hunt.

'What do you want me to do?' Betsy began to tumble the silver back into the box.

Mrs Jeffries thought for a few moments. There were so many loose ends, so many tiny clues that might or might not be worth pursuing. Suddenly Antonia Everdene's pinched face flashed into her mind. 'I want you to go to the Everdene house in Putney. See if you can find a housemaid or a footman and find out every little detail about the time Mary spent there.'

Betsy nodded eagerly, picked up the silver box and jammed it into the cupboard. She was dashing towards the kitchen stairs when Mrs Jeffries called her back.

'Betsy, be sure and find out if any of the servants overheard what Antonia Everdene said to Mary when she sacked her.'

'What if none of them was listenin'?'

'Oh, really, Betsy,' Mrs Jeffries admonished. 'Do you think that's likely?'

The maid grinned and tossed her blonde curls. 'No, but on behalf of the servin' classes, I felt I ought to say it.'

Mrs Goodge turned toward the kettle. 'I'd best

get ready, then. The boy'll be here in a few minutes to pick up the laundry, and there's a chimney sweep comin' into Mrs Gaines's house next door. We've got a delivery of fish expected as well, and ol' Thomas, the rag-and-bone man, is usually around these parts late in the day.' She glanced up at Mrs Jeffries as she filled the kettle. 'Is there anything in particular you want me to be diggin' for?'

Again Mrs Jeffries had to stop and think. This case was getting so complicated, she wasn't sure what was important and what wasn't. But she certainly didn't want the cook wasting any precious gossip opportunities just because she couldn't determine the next course of action. She decided to err on the side of caution. One could never learn too much about the people involved in a victim's life. 'See if you can learn anything else about the Lutterbanks. Concentrate your efforts on Andrew Lutterbank, and see if you can ferret out any more details about that scandal with that young girl who was sent off to Australia.'

'What about the Everdenes?'

'Find out what you can about Antonia Everdene's engagement,' Mrs Jeffries replied. 'See if anyone knows how Miss Everdene met her fiancé and more importantly where she met him. And see if anyone knows anything about Cassie Yates.'

'Her?' Mrs Goodge said in surprise. 'What are we wastin' our time on her for?'

Mrs Jeffries hesitated. 'I'm not really sure, Mrs Goodge. But I've a feeling she might be important. She may have seen or heard something that will give us a clue to who killed Mary. Anyway, it's worth trying.'

'What do you want me to find out?'

'Oh, let's see now. Why don't you ask about the facts? Find out where she's from, what her background is, whether or not she ever left any of her other employers and under what circumstances. That sort of thing.'

Mrs Goodge nodded, and Mrs Jeffries headed up to her rooms. She needed to sit down and think.

CHAPTER SEVEN

INSPECTOR WITHERSPOON WISHED he'd gone home for lunch. A nice, calm meal with his housekeeper would have been just the sort of activity he needed to get rid of this pounding headache. Instead, he'd gone back to Scotland Yard and heard another unsettling bit of information about this wretched case. Beside him, Constable Barnes shuffled his feet. Witherspoon gave him a weary smile. 'It shouldn't be much longer, Constable. I daresay this house isn't that large. The butler should be back any moment with Malcolm Farnsworth.'

They were standing in the opulent drawing room of Emery Clements's home in Kensington.

'Do you think that young Dr Bosworth knows what he's talking about?' Barnes asked. He kept his gaze on the open doorway. 'After all, he did admit he wasn't sure.'

'I don't really know, Constable,' Witherspoon admitted. 'But I'm inclined to take the view that it's possible. Medical science is advancing further every day, and if Dr Bosworth thinks the girl might have been pregnant, then we'll assume he's correct.'

'But even he said he couldn't say for certain,' Barnes argued.

'True. The internal organs were badly decomposed, but Bosworth strikes me as an intelligent young fellow.' Witherspoon didn't need to add that he thought Dr Potter was a pompous fool – his constable already knew that.

'But coming to the conclusion the girl had a bun in her oven just from lookin' at a few bits and pieces of her insides under that . . . that . . . What was the name of that thing he was going on about?'

'A microscope.'

'That's it. Well, I tell you, it ain't right.' Barnes shook his head. 'How could he see if she was expectin' or not just from looking at her innards?'

'Bosworth merely said that when he examined her internal organs under the microscope, there was some indication that she might have been with child.' Witherspoon shrugged. 'It's not the sort of evidence we could ever use in court, of course. But let's face it, Barnes, we're at the point in this investigation when any little bit helps. At the very least, perhaps the pregnancy was a motive for murder.'

'That's true.' Barnes agreed grudgingly. 'It wouldn't be the first time a man's got rid of an unwanted burden by killin' it. But the whole idea gives me the willies. It's bad enough to think of some poor pregnant girl gettin' murdered, but then to have her insides poked and prodded about by some fool doctor, and all in the name of science too.'

'Now, now, Constable.' Witherspoon glanced at the door again. 'Dr Bosworth was only doing what he thought was right. He didn't have to come to us at all and took a substantial risk by telling us his suspicions. We both know that Dr Potter certainly wouldn't have appreciated Dr Bosworth's interference. Potter's notoriously territorial about post-mortems.'

'Humph. Not that it does us much good, even if Bosworth's right. Pregnant or not, we still don't know who she is.'

They both turned at the sound of footsteps. Witherspoon stared at the tall, fair-haired young man entering the room. He was somewhat overdressed for the afternoon, in a pristine white shirt, dark blue coat, fashionable waistcoat and brilliant crimson cravat. His handsome features were composed in an expression of cautious interest, but the bright blue eyes beneath his long, dark lashes were wary.

'Good afternoon, gentlemen,' he said forcefully as he advanced across the room. 'I'm Malcolm Farnsworth. My butler said you wanted to have a word with me.'

'Good afternoon, sir.' Witherspoon inclined his head in acknowledgment of the introduction. 'I'm Inspector Witherspoon of Scotland Yard, and this is Constable Barnes.'

Farnsworth smiled slightly. 'May I ask what this is all about?'

'My constable and I have had a hard morning, sir,' the inspector replied, knowing that Barnes's feet were probably hurting him. 'May we sit down?'

'Certainly.' Farnsworth waved a hand towards a settee, and the matching wing chairs. Everyone sat down. 'Now, could you please tell me why you're here?'

Witherspoon reached into his pocket and fished out

the ring. He handed it to Farnsworth. 'Can you identify this betrothal ring as one you purchased?'

'Egad. Where on earth did you find this?' Farnsworth smiled in delight. 'I must say, I'm very impressed. It never occurred to me that Scotland Yard would trouble themselves over such a trifle. Not that it wasn't expensive, mind you. It jolly well was, but I hardly thought a lost ring would be of much concern to the police. I say, how did you know it was mine? I never reported losing it.'

The inspector shot a quick glance at Barnes, who peered up from his notebook with an expression of surprise.

'Are you saying you lost this object?'

'By heavens, yes. You chaps must be frightfully clever to find it.' Farnsworth chuckled. 'I must say, it put me in a decidedly awkward position.'

Witherspoon was disappointed. 'In what way, Mr Farnsworth?'

'Well, here I was, getting ready to ask my fiancée for her hand in marriage, and when I reached into my pocket for the ring, the wretched thing was gone.' He leaned forward and smiled conspiratorially. 'You know how the ladies are, Inspector. It was dreadfully embarrassing. Of course, Antonia pretended not to notice anything was wrong, and I hardly felt like admitting that I'd done something so silly as to lose her engagement ring.'

Witherspoon hadn't the least idea how the ladies were, but he refrained from saying so. Instead, he forced himself to concentrate. 'When did all this happen? I mean, when did you realize it was gone?'

'As I've just said,' Farnsworth replied huffily, 'I realized the ring was gone when I went to put it on my fiancée's finger.'

'And exactly when would that have been?'

'Do you want the date?' Farnsworth asked. At the inspector's nod, he lifted one long, elegant hand to his chin and his eyes narrowed in concentration. 'I believe it was sometime in early September,' he answered slowly. 'Perhaps the tenth or the eleventh, but I can't be certain.'

'You can't remember the date you got engaged, sir?' Barnes asked.

'Well, no.' Farnsworth gave the constable a puzzled frown. 'That's the sort of thing a woman remembers, not a man. I say, Inspector. What's this all about?'

Witherspoon waited a moment before answering. 'Murder.'

'Murder! My God, how dreadful. But what does it have to do with this ring?' Farnsworth gulped and looked down at his hand. As he stared at the tiny band, a wave of colour washed over his cheeks and he shuddered slightly. Witherspoon coughed softly, and Farnsworth quickly handed him the ring.

'It was found on the body of the victim,' the inspector replied. He slipped the ring back into his pocket. 'She'd been stabbed and then buried in the cellar of a house on Magpie Lane. Do you know the place?'

Farnsworth clamped his hands together. 'No.'

'Strange. The property is owned by Mr Emery Clements. There was considerable controversy over those houses, some sort of dispute about whether a road would be built or a new underground line dug.

135

As you live with Mr Clements, I'm surprised you never heard him mention Magpie Lane.'

'Mr Clements's company has property all over England,' Farnsworth replied, but his voice was noticeably less strong than before. 'I can hardly be expected to recall every little detail of those properties which are causing him difficulties. It happens all the time.'

'I see.' Witherspoon studied the man carefully. The mention of murder had shaken him to his core. Gone was the confident voice and the ready smile. Farnsworth was white as a sheet and was having to twine his fingers together to keep them from shaking. He was hiding something, but what? 'Do you have any idea who the young lady was?'

'What young lady?'

'The victim.'

'Don't be absurd, man.' Farnsworth swelled with indignation. 'How on earth would I know such a thing? I've told you, I lost that wretched ring on the day I asked my fiancée to marry me. For all I know, my pocket might have been picked! It's not as if you fellows are much good at protecting innocent citizens from thieves and pickpockets.'

'Exactly where did you go on that day?' Barnes asked softly. 'It would be helpful if we knew exactly where you lost it.'

The question appeared to startle Farnsworth for a moment. 'Lord. I've no idea. Could you remember what you did on any particular day two months ago?'

'I could if I'd just asked a young lady to be my wife,' Barnes replied firmly. 'And if I'd lost the expensive engagement ring I'd bought to put on her finger.'

'Well, obviously, I'm not as romantic as you appear to be, Constable. Except for asking Antonia to marry me, it was a day like any other.' Farnsworth leapt to his feet and began pacing in front of the marble fireplace.

'Perhaps if you'd tell us how you generally spend your days,' Witherspoon said, trying to be helpful. 'Perhaps that would nudge your memory a tad.'

Farnsworth stopped pacing and turned to stare at the inspector, his expression sceptical. After a moment, he shrugged. 'Oh, all right, but I think it's useless. Normally, I get up and breakfast with Emery. I spend an hour or two after that in my rooms; then I frequently accompany Mrs Clements on a walk. After luncheon, I generally go to my club or to visit friends. I spend my evenings in much the same way.'

'When do you see your fiancée, sir?' Barnes asked.

Farnsworth looked offended. 'That's hardly any of Scotland Yard's concern. But if you must know, I see Antonia quite frequently. And I'm afraid this little exercise has been pointless. The only thing I can remember about the day I lost the ring is just as I've told you. It wasn't there when I reached into my pocket.'

'Your fiancée is a Miss Antonia Everdene,' Witherspoon said. It was a statement, not a question.

'How do you know that?'

'Mr Clements told us,' the inspector replied. 'We saw him earlier today. That's how we traced the ring to you. Mr Clements identified it as one you'd purchased on his account at Broghan's. Is that correct?'

'Yes.' Farnsworth flushed a dull red and looked away.

Witherspoon gazed at him sympathetically. It must be terribly humiliating to have to obtain a loan to buy one's fiancée a ring. And then to have that fact become public knowledge. Well, the inspector could understand the gentleman's embarrassment. He got up, and so did Constable Barnes. 'I'd like to have a word with Mrs Clements, if I may,' he said.

'That's impossible,' Farnsworth replied. He looked quickly towards the open door. 'She can tell you nothing. Mrs Clements is a very elderly lady, and she's resting. You'll have to come back tomorrow. If I were you, I should do it when Mr Clements is here.'

Barnes and Witherspoon exchanged glances.

'Yes, perhaps you're right,' Witherspoon said. 'Could you give us Miss Everdene's address?'

'Why do you want her address?' Farnsworth asked in alarm. 'I tell you Antonia knows nothing of this murder. I won't have you bothering her with such nonsense!'

'Murder is hardly nonsense,' the inspector replied softly. 'And I assure you, sir, we will do our best not to upset Miss Everdene.'

Farnsworth sighed. 'All right, if it's absolutely necessary. But I must warn you, Antonia's very delicate. She lives at number three Harcourt Lane, in Putney.'

The inspector thought of the young woman who'd lain buried in a dark, dirty cellar for two months. Perhaps she'd been a delicate woman too, yet no one seemed overly concerned with her.

'Perhaps Miss Everdene can recall the exact date you proposed to her,' Barnes interjected with a sly smile. 'As you said, Mr Farnsworth, that's the sort of thing a woman remembers.'

★　★　★

The inspector had just finished telling Mrs Jeffries the details of his day when she hastily excused herself to answer the front door.

A few moments later, he stifled a groan as his house-keeper returned, followed by Luty Belle Crookshank. He'd been so looking forward to eating his dinner in peace.

'Howdy, Inspector,' Luty said. 'Now don't you be fretting that I'm gonna take a lot of your time. I jes needs to have quick word about that body you found in Magpie Lane.'

'Please sit down, Mrs Crookshank,' Witherspoon responded as he leapt up and ushered the elderly lady to his favourite chair. 'It's always a pleasure to see you,' he lied gallantly, not wanting to hurt the dear lady's feelings. 'And don't worry about taking my time – I'm not in the least concerned about how much of my time you need. Now, what's all this about?'

'Well,' Luty spread the skirts of her scarlet satin dress more comfortably around her feet. 'I've been thinkin' I mighta been wrong the other day.'

'Wrong? In what way?'

'People see what's they want to see, Inspector.' Luty glanced at Mrs Jeffries, who gave her a reassuring smile. 'And I'm thinkin' when I told you that body weren't Mary, I mighta made a mistake.'

'Now you think it is Mary?' Witherspoon didn't know whether to be elated or depressed.

'Well, it's like this. I've learned a few things . . . No offence meant, Inspector, but when Mary plum disappeared the way she did, I went out and hired me an inquiry agent.'

'An inquiry agent?'

Luty nodded her head. 'Yup. An American inquiry feller, used to know him in San Francisco. Name's Braxton Paxton. Silly name but a smart man. He's a mighty fine snoop too. Well, it only took him a few days of pryin' around to find out all sorts of interestin' things.'

'Really? Gracious, what did this Mr Baxton learn?'

'Paxton,' Luty corrected. 'And he learned enough to make me think I mighta made a mistake about that body you showed me.'

For the next half hour, Luty told the inspector every detail the servants of upper Edmonton Gardens had learned in the course of their investigations.

She told him about Mary's disappearance, the missing brooch, the Lutterbanks, the Everdenes and even the odd bits of gossip about Sally Comstock and Andrew Lutterbank. Finally, she told him about Cassie Yates.

Witherspoon listened attentively, occasionally asking a question. If he wasn't asking the right questions, Mrs Jeffries would interject one, just to make sure he was getting the point.

'My word,' Witherspoon finally said, when Luty Belle had finished. 'You've found out an enormous amount of detail. I say, I'd really like to have a word with this Mr Caxton.'

'His name's Paxton, but you can't talk to him.' Luty smiled innocently. 'He's gone to France to work on a problem for some winemaker. Don't know why. The French are about the snootiest bodies on the face of the earth. But that's Paxton for ya. He goes anywhere there's trouble. Why, back in sixty-eight he single-handedly stopped the biggest shanghai operation on the coast. Had half the scum of San Francisco on his tail that time, and he didn't turn a hair.'

Mrs Jeffries shot Luty a warning glance, but the elderly woman just gave her a guileless smile and got up. 'I've got to be goin' now,' she said. 'It's gettin' late and I want to git home.' Witherspoon started to get up too, but she waved him back in his chair. 'Don't trouble yerself to see me to the door. I kin find my own way.'

'I'll see you to the door,' Mrs Jeffries announced. She took Luty firmly by the arm, and when they reached the hall, she leaned over and hissed in her ear, 'Now really, Luty. Don't you think you were overdoing it a bit in there? The inspector's no fool. Gone to France, indeed. And where did you come up with that peculiar name?'

'I didn't make that name up,' Luty said defensively. 'There really is a Braxton Paxton. Course I wouldn't exactly call him a detective, more like a fix-it man, if you ask me. He used to do a lot of jobs for some of the cattle ranchers and shipping companies back in San Francisco.'

'Not to worry then,' Mrs Jeffries said soothingly. 'You were quite right. If the inspector does do any checking on Mr Paxton, he'll find he exists.' She stopped by the front door and smiled. 'You did well, Luty. I know it couldn't have been easy for you. But we'll find whoever killed Mary. I promise you.'

Luty stared at her for a moment, her black eyes unreadable in the glow of the gas lamps. 'I'm still not so sure that Mary is the one that's dead.' She held up her hand when she saw Mrs Jeffries open her mouth to protest. 'Don't go gettin' all het up, Hepzibah. I ain't askin' you to waste any more time lookin' for the girl, not when there's a murderer runnin' around out there. But I got me this feelin' . . .' She broke off. 'Leastways, I won't really believe she's dead until we catch whoever done it and they admit it from their own lips. But until then, I ain't givin' up hope.'

Over dinner, Mrs Jeffries wondered whether she should have told Luty about the possibility of Mary having been pregnant. But as the inspector himself hadn't been sure of that particular fact, she decided she'd done the right thing.

The inspector discussed the case freely. Mrs Jeffries made sure that everything he'd heard from Luty Belle was planted firmly in his mind. In turn, she deftly managed to make him repeat everything he'd learned from Emery Clements and Malcolm Farnsworth. She made it a point to emphasize the fact that both Clements and Farnsworth were frequent visitors to the Lutterbank house and therefore had to have known Mary Sparks.

By the time dinner was finished, she was eager to get down to the kitchen. Betsy, Smythe and Wiggins should be back by now. She flushed guiltily as she remembered the tiny white lie she'd told to explain the maid's absence. Inspector Witherspoon thought Betsy was at a Methodist Ladies Temperance meeting. She must remember to share that fact with Betsy too.

She was the only one who'd returned. She and Mrs Goodge were just finishing their own dinner when Mrs Jeffries came into the kitchen.

'There weren't no one home at the Everdenes',' Betsy said as Mrs Jeffries stepped up to the table. 'So I went back to Knightsbridge to see if I could learn a bit more about Mary or Cassie. Was that all right?'

'Of course it was,' Mrs Jeffries replied. She frowned at the two empty places where Smythe and Wiggins should have been sitting.

Betsy caught the housekeeper's anxious expression. 'It's past nine o'clock and they're not back yet,' she burst out. 'And I'm startin' to get real fidgety over it.'

So was Mrs Jeffries. She didn't worry all that much about the coachman – he could take care of himself. But it certainly wasn't like Wiggins to be late. 'Now Betsy,' she said calmly, 'I'm sure they'll be here any moment. Worrying won't do any of us any good.'

'It's not like Wiggins to be late,' Mrs Goodge said darkly. 'Something's wrong. He'd sooner give up mooning over one of those silly girls than miss his dinner.'

'We don't know that anything is wrong,' Mrs Jeffries said firmly. She hesitated, not sure what to do next. 'But it would be pointless to start discussing the case now and then have to repeat ourselves when those two finally show up. Why don't we give them an hour or two? We can meet back here later for cocoa. Is that agreeable to everyone?'

Betsy sighed and nodded. 'I don't feel much like talkin' now, that's for certain. Without the others 'ere, it wouldn't seem right.'

'I agree.' Mrs Goodge heaved herself out of her chair and reached for her empty plate. 'I don't much like havin' to repeat myself.'

'All right, then. We'll meet here at ten o'clock.' Mrs Jeffries forced herself to smile. 'I'm sure both Smythe and Wiggins will be here by then, and they'll have all sorts of interesting facts to report.'

'But what if they're not?' Betsy asked anxiously. 'What'll we do?'

'If they're not back,' Mrs Jeffries said firmly, 'we'll start looking for them.'

'What? Us? Start lookin'?' Mrs Goodge said incredulously, clearly appalled at the thought of leaving her kitchen.

'Yes, us. If we have to, we'll wake the inspector and we'll get some of Luty Belle's servants to help.' Mrs Jeffries lifted her chin. 'But I'm sure it won't come to that. Nothing has happened to either of them. Smythe's more than capable of taking care of himself, and Wiggins, despite occasional actions to the contrary, isn't a fool.'

For the next hour, Mrs Jeffries paced her room. She tried to concentrate on the facts she had about the murder, but it was so hard to think. She was too worried about the missing men. Especially about Wiggins.

Stopping in front of her window, she stared out at the night sky and tried to put her finger on precisely what was bothering her. But the task was hopeless. There was no reason for her to be so anxious. No doubt Wiggins would turn up safe and sound and with a perfectly good explanation for his absence. It wasn't as if this case were peopled with desperate killers brandishing knives and pistols. Then she realized what she'd just thought and remembered that Mary Sparks had been stabbed.

Perhaps whoever had killed Mary had found out

Wiggins was investigating the crime. But how could that be? The only place Wiggins went was Knightsbridge and from there to Garrett McGraw's home. So how could anyone know what he was up to?

But maybe someone had seen him lurking about the gardens? But who? Andrew Lutterbank? He was a definite possibility – he lived there. Or Emery Clements and Malcolm Farnsworth? They were friends of Andrew's. Or perhaps even one of the other servants, someone who had a grudge against Mary and then realized that Wiggins was following the one lead they had to the girl . . . Oh, drat, Mrs Jeffries thought disgustedly, this is getting me nowhere.

With sheer willpower, she went to her desk and pulled out a piece of paper. Taking up her pen, she began writing down the details of the case she'd learned so far.

As soon as she'd finished, she picked the paper up and read it through. Her spirits sank. All she had was a useless list of facts, dates and rumours. There was no murder weapon; there were no witnesses – no nothing. There wasn't a clue as to who the killer was, and even more disheartening, there wasn't a thing on the paper that gave her any idea of why Mary had been murdered. And until they understood the why of it, she had a feeling they'd never discover the who.

They met in the kitchen at exactly ten o'clock. The two men still weren't home. Mrs Goodge had made cocoa and put out a plate of buns. 'Right,' she said briskly as she slammed a mug down in front of her. 'Who wants to get the inspector?'

'I expect I'd better,' Mrs Jeffries said. She was interrupted by a soft knock on the back door. Betsy jumped to her feet so quickly her chair fell over with a crash, but she ignored it and raced for the door.

'Ask who it is,' the housekeeper warned, but she was too late. Betsy had already pulled the door wide.

'Well, good evenin', darlin'.' A smiling redheaded giant of a man stepped into the kitchen. 'Wiggins didn't say I'd be meetin' one so fair as you, now. But then, I'm not surprised. 'E's no doubt keepin' you all to himself, and who could blame a man for that?'

Startled, Betsy stared at the man as if he had two heads. ' 'Ho are you?' she exclaimed, so surprised she reverted to her old way of speaking.

Mrs Jeffries stood up. 'Yes, I believe introductions are in order.'

The man swept off a rather grimy flat cap and bowed to the ladies. 'Pardon me, madam. My name is Fletcher Beaks. I'm a friend of Wiggins's. I've brought a message from him. He was afraid you'd be a bit worried, now.'

Mrs Goodge eyed the smiling giant warily. 'We have been a mite anxious,' she mumbled.

Fletcher Beaks stood a good six and a half feet tall, with shoulder-length carrot-red hair, a ruddy complexion and pale blue eyes. He was dressed in dark trousers, a white shirt with full sleeves and a pin-striped waistcoat. Over one of his large arms he carried a brown cloak.

'Well, we're glad Wiggins finally decided to get in touch with us,' Mrs Jeffries said. Knowing she was being rude, she tried hard not to stare. 'Please come in and sit down, Mr Beaks.'

Betsy finally gathered her wits and rushed back to

the table, stopping to pick up the chair she'd over-turned. Fletcher Beaks, his eyes following the maid's every movement, trailed behind her. He took the chair Mrs Jeffries indicated.

'Thank you, ma'am,' he said with a wide grin, his eyes riveted on Betsy.

Mrs Goodge cleared her throat. 'Would you care for some cocoa?' she asked.

'No, thank you.' Reluctantly, he tore his gaze away from the maid. 'Much as I'd love to stay and revel in your charmin' company,' he said to the table at large, 'I've only got a minute or two. I'll just deliver my message and be on my way. But perhaps you'll take pity on a poor lonely fellow like myself and invite me round another time.'

'Yes, I'm sure we will,' Mrs Jeffries said hastily. 'Now, what is the message?'

'Wiggins told me to tell you that he's hot on the trail and not to worry,' Fletcher Beaks said. 'By tomorrow morning, he should find what he's looking for.'

Mrs Jeffries smiled. 'Where is Wiggins?'

'As to that, I can't say.' He shrugged. 'The last time I saw the lad, he was running down Dunsany Road.'

'Where's that?' Betsy asked.

'Hammersmith.' Fletcher's smile widened as he turned and gazed at Betsy.

'Hammersmith?' Mrs Goodge frowned. 'What's he doin' in that part of town?'

'I really don't know.' Keeping his gaze on Betsy, who was now blushing a furious red, Fletcher got up. 'But as I owe the boy a favour or two, I was delighted to bring his message. Now, much as I'd like to stay and talk with you lovely ladies, I really must be off. I've got to get to work.'

He bowed formally, put on his hat and left.

'Well, at least we know that Wiggins is all right,' Mrs Jeffries said as the back door closed behind their mysterious visitor.

'But what about Smythe?' Betsy said. ''Ow come he's not 'ere?'

'Perhaps he too is "hot on the trail",' Mrs Jeffries suggested hopefully. 'Besides, as we've said before, Smythe can take care of himself.'

'Not if some killer's stuck a knife in 'im!' Betsy protested.

'Oh, get on with you, girl,' Mrs Goodge snapped. 'No one's gonna be stickin' nothing in Smythe except a pint of bitter, and he'll be gettin' that from some barman. Stop yer frettin', and let's get on with this. I've found out somethin'.'

'Excellent,' Mrs Jeffries said.

'But I thought we were going to wait for the others,' Betsy wailed.

'We don't have time,' Mrs Jeffries replied. She turned to Mrs Goodge. 'Go on.'

'I've found out that Andrew Lutterbank's been virtually cut off.' Mrs Goodge crossed her arms in front of her and rested them on the table. 'He still lives at the house in Knightsbridge, but his father won't have much to do with him. Exceptin' for spendin' an occasional weekend at some little cottage he's got out in the country somewhere, he's practically a prisoner.'

'But why?' Betsy asked. 'If he's been disinherited, 'ow come he's still livin' at 'ome?'

''Cause he don't have nowhere else to go nor any money.' The cook reached for a bun. 'And he can't get employment. Seems his reputation is too unsavoury for them that employs gentlemen.'

'Why was he disinherited,' Mrs Jeffries asked eagerly, 'and more importantly, do you know when?'

'The best I could find out was that his father was finally fed up with 'im seducin' housemaids and leavin' his bastards everywhere. The last time it happened was with that girl,' she broke off, trying to remember the name.

'Sally Comstock?' Mrs Jeffries supplied.

'That's her. Anyway, it seems that when he got her in trouble, his father paid the girl off with a big wad of money. Money that was Andrew's quarterly allowance. Then he told young Andrew he was tired of such behaviour and that the boy couldn't expect to inherit anything from him.' Mrs Goodge laughed cynically. 'But blood's thicker than water, and I reckon one of the reasons the boy's still livin' at home is in hopes of softening the old man up.'

'That's right strange, you know,' Betsy said thoughtfully.

'What is?' Mrs Jeffries poured out a cup of chocolate.

'Well, I 'appened to find out that Cassie Yates, when she was workin' at the Lutterbanks, shared a room with Sally Comstock.' She broke off and laughed. 'As a matter of fact, the only nice thing I've heard about Cassie at all was that she'd snuck out the night Sally left – she told everyone she wanted to say goodbye to her friend.' Betsy shrugged. 'Jus' goes to show that everyone's got some little bit of good in 'em, don't it?'

'Indeed it does, Betsy.' Mrs Jeffries turned back to the cook. 'Did you find out when the Comstock girl left?'

'No, but it should be easy enough to check. She left right after old Angus Lutterbank's funeral. Mr Lutterbank was so angry with Andrew that as soon as the service was over, he made the boy take the girl straight down to the docks and put her on the ship to Australia himself. We can check at St Matthew's for the date of the funeral.'

'Why are you so interested in Sally Comstock?' Betsy asked curiously. 'Mary weren't even workin' at the Lutterbanks' when Sally was there.'

'I'm not sure,' Mrs Jeffries confessed. 'Curiosity, I suppose. Now, what did you find out?'

'Not much really,' Betsy admitted. 'But I did find out the name of the man who was Cassie Yates's third admirer. It were Andrew Lutterbank himself. But he must have learned his lesson 'cause the girl I was talkin' to told me that Andrew took care only to meet with Cassie away from the house.'

'Then how did she find out?' Mrs Goodge asked.

'She saw Cassie and Andrew together twice. They met in the park. Oh, and there's no record of Cassie gettin' married at any of the local churches, and none of the girls I talked to 'ad any idea where it could have taken place.' Betsy turned to Mrs Jeffries. 'Do you want me to keep lookin'?'

'I'm not sure, Betsy,' Mrs Jeffries confessed. 'Wait until you hear what I've learned today, and then we'll decide what to do next.'

She told them all about Emery Clements and

Malcolm Farnsworth. She gave them the details of Luty Belle's visit and said that Witherspoon had mentioned he was going to the Everdene house tomorrow. She then told them about Dr Bosworth's theory that the victim had been pregnant.

'Pregnant?' Betsy gasped. 'But that doesn't sound like Mary at all.'

'The behaviour Antonia Everdene described to me didn't sound like Mary either,' Mrs Jeffries said earnestly. 'Yet we know she went there that day and started work. But nothing makes sense in this case so far. However, we won't give up until we uncover the truth.' For a moment she was tempted to quote Mr Walt Whitman, the American poet. She couldn't quite remember the verse, but it was something about looking until one really saw. And that's just what they'd keep doing too. She turned to Betsy and said, 'Will you be able to get to Putney tomorrow? I think it's rather important that we find out what happened between Antonia Everdene and Mary.'

'I'll go first thing in the morning.'

'Be careful that you don't run into the inspector,' Mrs Jeffries warned. The back door slammed and startled her so that she jumped.

'Cor, it's about time you got 'ere,' Betsy shouted.

Turning, Mrs Jeffries saw Smythe. He gave her a cocky smile and swaggered to the table like the king of the mountain.

CHAPTER EIGHT

'GOOD EVENING, SMYTHE,' Mrs Jeffries said pleasantly. 'We've been a bit concerned about you.'

'There was no need for that,' he replied, giving Mrs Goodge a wink and pulling out a chair. 'You knows I can take care of myself.'

'Not when there's a murderer runnin' around stickin' knives in people's 'earts,' Betsy snapped. 'Worryin' us to death was right inconsiderate.'

The coachman looked startled. 'Now, now, lass,' he began soothingly. 'I weren't doin' it a purpose, but I was in the thick o' things and couldn't get back.'

Mrs Goodge snorted and Betsy narrowed her eyes. Mrs Jeffries quickly intervened. 'Well, now that you are back, perhaps you'd be so kind as to tell us what you've been up to.'

Smythe reached for the pot of cocoa, poured himself some and leaned back in his chair. 'Where's Wiggins?'

'He's hot on the trail,' Betsy said sarcastically, taking care to enunciate every word. 'Like you, I guess he can't be bothered with comin' 'ome either.'

'Look I've already told ya—' he began defensively, but Mrs Jeffries cut him off.

'Yes, we know what you've told us,' she said. 'Now we're wasting time here. We've learned a lot since you've been gone, and we need to know what you've found out.'

'I finally found the bloke that drove the hired coach from Cassie Yates's lodgin's. That's why I've been gone so long.' He smiled smugly and took a long, leisurely sip from his mug.

Betsy sighed, Mrs Goodge rolled her eyes and even Mrs Jeffries was tempted to give him a swift kick in the leg; instead she gave him what he wanted to hear. 'We knew you'd catch up with the fellow sooner or later. You're very clever, Smythe.'

He leaned forward on his elbows, his dark brown eyes shining. 'The man that come for Cassie's belongin's were a tall, well-dressed feller who paid double the regular 'irin' price – seems he were in a 'urry that mornin' and didn't want to wait around for one of the other coaches to come back. He paid twice what was needed to take a coach and driver out that were already promised to someone else.'

'Who was the man?' Mrs Jeffries asked.

'He never give a name, and he took some pains to disguise 'imself. Mitchell, that's the man that drove the coach that day, said 'e wore a fancy top hat and a scarf around 'is neck to cover his face.'

'We already know that,' Betsy said waspishly, letting them know, less than tactfully, that she'd already reported this particular fact two days ago.

Smythe frowned impatiently. 'Yes, but what you

don't know is 'ow strange the feller acted. On the mornin' of the eleventh, he ordered the driver to go to the girl's house. 'E tipped the landlady nice and then went inside. 'Alf an hour later, he come out loaded down with a carpetbag and boxes and the like. Now this is where it starts to get interestin'. Mitchell 'urried over to give the man a bit o' 'elp, but the bloke was 'avin' none of that. He ordered the driver back onto the coach, loaded Cassie's things inside 'imself and then told the man to drive on.'

'What's so interestin' about that?' Betsy asked archly.

Instead of taking offence at her sneering tone, Smythe turned and gave her a long, thoughtful stare.

'It's interesting because by rights, the man who 'ired the coach shouldn't have lifted a finger to do any of the work,' Mrs Goodge explained.

'True,' Mrs Jeffries added. 'Generally, the driver does all the carting and loading, but in this case, who- ever hired that coach didn't want the driver anywhere near either Cassie's rooms or Cassie's things.'

'Oh.' Betsy flushed slightly.

Smythe grinned. 'But that's not all that's odd 'ere,' he continued. 'Once the bloke was back in the coach, 'e ordered the driver to take 'im out of London, to a small village in Essex. Once they got there, the same thing 'appened. The driver just sat there while the man unloaded Cassie's belongin's.'

'Was Cassie there?'

'Not 'ide nor 'air of 'er,' Smythe said firmly. 'The reason I were so late gettin' in tonight were because I been out to the place.'

'Did you manage to get inside?' Mrs Jeffries asked.

'Couldn't,' he admitted with a shake of his head. 'The place were locked up tighter than a bank vault, but I got a good gander in the windows, and no one's been there in months. The man just left 'er belongin's piled in a 'eap in the parlour, but there's dust and cobwebs everywhere.'

Mrs Goodge poured Smythe more cocoa. 'Who does the place belong to?'

'It don't rightly belong to any one person,' the coachman confessed. 'The cottage sits on less than an acre of its own ground. Accordin' to one of the neighbours, it were sold last year to a London property company.'

Mrs Jeffries's eyes met Smythe's. 'Wildwoods'. It was a statement, not a question. She wasn't surprised when he slowly nodded.

'Yes. I found that out from one of the neighbours. But no one can figure out what they want with a piddly bit o' land and a tumbledown cottage.'

'What did the man do after he'd taken in Cassie's things?' Betsy asked. She seemed eager to redeem herself.

''E got back in the coach, and they drove back to town. The driver left 'im off at Hyde Park, and that were the last 'e saw of 'im. Except the man give 'im 'alf a crown.'

'You've done very well, Smythe,' Mrs Jeffries said. 'Now I do believe we'd better bring you up to date on what we've learned in your absence.'

She gave him the information, leaving nothing out and stressing Betsy's contribution. She also told him about the missing Wiggins and the mysterious message. When she'd finished, the coachman's normally cheeky expression had been replaced with a heavy frown.

155

'Good gracious, you look like you've just bitten into a sour apple,' Mrs Jeffries exclaimed. 'What's wrong?'

'I'm not sure,' he said slowly, 'but I'm not likin' the feel o' this case. And I don't much like the fact that Wiggins is off by 'imself gettin' into mischief. The lad's good-hearted, but let's be blunt, Mrs J, sometimes 'e's got about as much sense as a lump of Mrs Goodge's bread dough.'

'That's not true,' the cook snapped. 'Wiggins might moon about a bit every now and again over some girl, but the boy's no fool.'

'I'm not sayin' 'e's a fool,' Smythe argued. 'I'm sayin' I'm worried. There's too many 'orses in this stable, too many bits and pieces we don't know.'

Smythe's attitude began to affect them all. Mrs Goodge bit her lip, Betsy began twisting one of her long blonde curls, and even Mrs Jeffries had to fight the urge to get up and start pacing. Smythe wasn't an alarmist.

'What particularly worries you so much?' Mrs Jeffries finally asked.

'Everythin'. Don't you see, the driver didn't get a look at the man . . . He were deliberately 'idin' his face.'

'But Cassie isn't the one that's dead. Mary is,' Betsy pointed out.

'Aye, Mary's dead and Cassie's missing, and there's at least three men who had something to do with both girls.'

Mrs Jeffries stifled a surge of panic as she grasped precisely what Smythe meant. 'You're right,' she said quietly, forcing herself to keep calm. 'But that doesn't mean we're dealing with a madman. The only thing we know for certain is that Mary is dead. We're only assuming that Cassie is missing because we haven't located her yet.'

'Madman?' Mrs Goodge yelped. 'Who said anythin' about a madman?'

Across the table, Smythe and Mrs Jeffries gazed at each other, their eyes grave, their expressions sombre.

'Are you two sayin' you think theys a lunatic killer runnin' about murderin' 'ousemaids?' Betsy glanced from the housekeeper to the coachman, then looked quizzically at the cook.

'Aye,' Smythe said slowly. 'That's exactly what I'm sayin', and I want you to start bein' a bit more careful . . .'

'Let's not jump to any conclusions,' Mrs Jeffries said firmly. 'We could easily be wrong. Mary is dead, but we don't know that there's anything in the least diabolical about Cassie Yates's disappearance. From what we've learned of that young lady's character, she could be off with some man.'

'Then 'ow come 'er belongin's is in that cottage and she ain't?' Smythe asked belligerently.

'Simple. The man might be married, and Cassie could have agreed to be his mistress,' Mrs Jeffries explained. 'She could have insisted he buy her new clothes. Oh, I don't know, but there are any one of a thousand reasons that could explain why he took her things to that cottage. But it's now imperative that we find out more.' She turned to Betsy. 'Don't bother with any of your chores tomorrow. I'll take care of dusting and cleaning the drawing room. Get over to Putney as early as you can and see if you can find out more about Mary's stay in the Everdene house.'

'I don't think that's a good idea,' Smythe said quickly. 'Shouldn't she stay 'ere and keep an eye out for Wiggins?'

'Don't be daft, man,' Betsy said with a sneer. 'I knows how to take care of meself too, and Mrs Goodge'll be 'ere when Wiggins finally sees fit to come 'ome.'

Smythe scowled at the girl but didn't bother to argue the point. He turned to Mrs Jeffries. 'I suppose you want me to see if I can find out what everyone was doin' on September the eleventh?'

Mrs Goodge slapped her hands flat against the table. 'Excuse me if I seem a bit slow,' she said sarcastically, 'but would someone mind tellin' me which three men we're talkin' about here?'

'Emery Clements, Malcolm Farnsworth and Andrew Lutterbank,' Mrs Jeffries said. 'Whoever took Cassie's things that day was probably one of those three, but we don't know which.'

'And why is that so important?' the cook enquired sourly, 'Mary's the one that's dead.'

Smythe sighed heavily, and Mrs Goodge glared at him.

'Because,' Mrs Jeffries intervened hastily, 'once we know who moved Cassie's things, we can find out once and for all if Cassie's all right.'

'You mean once we know that she's off livin' in sin, we can rest easier because we'll know we ain't dealin' with a lunatic,' Mrs Goodge finished smugly. 'Seems to me that's a waste of time. We'd be better concentratin' on what happened to Mary Sparks after she left the Everdene house.'

'That's precisely what Betsy is going to do.' Mrs Jeffries rose to her feet. 'And if you would be so kind, Mrs Goodge, do you think you could possibly find out the exact date of Angus Lutterbank's funeral? I'd like to know when Sally Comstock left for Australia. Supposedly, Andrew Lutterbank took her to the ship that night himself.'

'Why don't ya let me do that?' Smythe said as he rose to his feet. 'I can nip by St Matthew's tomorrow and have a word with the vicar. Then if you're really wantin' to find out if the girl left, I can pop down to the docks and nose around there. See if her name was on any passenger lists.'

Mrs Jeffries thought for a moment. 'Yes, that's a very good idea.'

'What'll I be doin' then?' the cook asked.

'Carry on as before,' Mrs Jeffries replied. 'Just keep asking your questions. You've turned up a great deal of useful information so far, and there's no reason to think the well's run dry at this point.' She paused and smiled kindly at Mrs Goodge, hoping the woman's feelings hadn't been hurt by the abrupt change in plans.

Mrs Goodge nodded. 'What are you goin' to be doin' next?'

'I've got the most difficult task of all,' Mrs Jeffries replied with a sigh. 'I'm going to have to think of a way to let the inspector know everything all of you have learned. That's not going to be easy.' She broke off and stared intently at the wall. 'But I think I might be able to drop a few hints at breakfast.'

'Do you want me to go out and 'ave a quick look round for Wiggins?' Smythe asked. He was staring at Betsy, who was gazing at the toe of her black shoe, barely visible beneath the hem of her grey housemaid's dress.

Betsy's head came up, and she smiled gratefully at the coachman. 'I think that's a right good notion,' she began excitedly. 'Even with gettin' a message from 'im, I don't think I'll sleep much knowin' he's not 'ome.'

Mrs Jeffries stared curiously at her two friends. She had the oddest feeling that Smythe had made the offer to keep Betsy from worrying. She watched as his broad, harsh face softened when he gazed down into the maid's eyes. But then she decided she must be mistaken as she heard his next words.

'Maybe I'll try a few of the pubs round Knightsbridge way,' he said, giving Betsy a cocky grin.

Betsy leapt to her feet. 'Pubs. Wiggins wouldn't go ta no pubs,' she exclaimed angrily. 'And 'ere I was thinkin' you was concerned, and all you want to do is go 'ave a few pints.'

'Give it a rest, lass.' He laughed and headed for the back door. 'I'm as concerned as the rest of you. And believe me, I'll come closer to findin' the boy by makin' me rounds than I would by skulkin' about in the streets.'

'Men.' Betsy gave an unladylike snort. 'They're all alike. If they ain't thinkin' of their stomachs, they're thinkin' of their drink. Disgustin'.'

There was nothing remotely spiritual or comforting about the Reverend Wendell Everdene, Witherspoon thought. He was a tall, barrel-chested bull of a man with a sallow complexion, a hawk's beak of a nose and a booming voice that reminded the inspector of a braying donkey. And from the way poor Barnes cringed slightly every time the reverend opened his mouth, Witherspoon imagined the constable's ears were probably ringing by now.

'Of all the impertinence, man,' Everdene bellowed. 'The girl was here for less than a day. I'm not surprised she's come to a bad end. That kind of creature always does. God will not be mocked. Sinful little chit, wouldn't allow her to sully the place.'

Constable Barnes winced. 'Are you saying, sir, that it was you who asked the girl to leave?'

Everdene's beady hazel eyes narrowed. 'What kind of a question is that? I'm the master of this house. The girl was a harlot. She had to go.'

'So you're confirming that you were, indeed, the one who actually asked her to leave?' Inspector Witherspoon wasn't terribly sure this was an important point, but he hadn't liked the way the man evaded answering Constable Barnes. In his experience, people who didn't give you a straight answer frequently had something to hide.

'I don't see that I need confirm anything.' Everdene glanced at his daughter. She was sitting rigidly in front of the fireplace, her thin lips pursed together and her hands neatly folded in her lap, the very picture of filial devotion.

'But we have it on good authority that it was Miss Everdene who fired Mary Sparks.' The inspector nodded politely to the lady. 'We understand that

Miss Sparks was behaving rather badly when Miss Everdene's fiancé arrived that evening and that Miss Everdene witnessed this behaviour. Shortly afterwards, she fired the girl. Isn't this true?'

'Absolutely not,' thundered the reverend. 'Who told you such wicked lies? My daughter was in the parlour when Malcolm arrived. I was the one who saw the disgraceful way the harlot behaved. I was the one that told her to get out. Antonia knew nothing about the matter till the next morning.'

''E's lyin' 'is bleedin' 'ead off,' the girl scoffed as she gently eased the door shut and turned to grin at Betsy.

Betsy smiled back at her and then glanced worriedly at the door the parlourmaid had just shut. She sincerely hoped that Inspector Witherspoon wouldn't take it into his head to search the house. There was no possible way she could explain being in the small pantry between the drawing room and dining room with Essie Tuttle.

Betsy couldn't believe her luck when she'd arrived at the Everdene house this morning and found most of the servants gone and a talkative parlourmaid who was more than willing to chat. But within minutes of her own arrival, Inspector Witherspoon and Constable Barnes had shown up.

Essie Tuttle, who didn't appear at all concerned about losing her position, had obligingly hurried the both of them into the pantry, opened the door a crack and then settled down to eavesdrop.

'How do you know 'e's lying?' Betsy whispered.

''Cause he were the one that was in the parlour,'

Essie replied. 'He was so soused he could barely walk. Mary coulda danced rings around 'im that night and he wouldna noticed.'

From the drawing room, Betsy heard Inspector Witherspoon point out that the betrothal ring found on Mary Sparks had been purchased for Antonia Everdene.

'Don't be absurd,' the reverend sneered. 'Malcolm knew Antonia wouldn't want a gaudy piece of jewellery like that. Not for something as sacred as marriage. He very rightly gave my daughter a small, plain band inscribed with the cross of our Lord. He showed it to me when he asked for my permission to wed the girl.'

Betsy stared in surprise. If she remembered correctly, Malcolm Farnsworth had claimed that when he showed up at the Everdenes' house, he didn't have a ring with him at all.

'He's lyin' again,' Essie giggled. 'Cor, for a preacher, it's a wonder his tongue ain't dropped off from all them lies.'

'What do you mean?' Betsy strained to listen but she didn't want the flow from Essie to dry up either.

'He's seen that ring afore this. I know 'cause I saw him kissin' Mary's hand and lookin' at it the day she come 'ere.'

'He was kissin' her hand?'

Essie laughed cynically. 'And everythin' else he could grab. She hadn't been in the 'ouse 'alf an 'our before the old lech was pawin' at 'er.'

Betsy opened her mouth to ask the maid how Mary had handled the reverend's advances, but before she could get the question out, she heard Inspector

Witherspoon ask Antonia Everdene if she'd ever seen the betrothal ring. Betsy cocked her ear in the direction of the drawing room.

'No, I've never seen it,' Antonia replied in a firm voice.

'She's a bloomin' liar too,' Essie said with a sneer. 'She's ruddy well seen that ring. Mary Sparks had it on her finger the night she was 'ere. When the mistress sacked 'er, she was holdin' her 'and up and laughin'.'

'You mean Mary showed the betrothal ring to Miss Everdene?'

'And that ain't all,' Essie said eagerly, bobbing her head. 'She laughed at the mistress, told her it would be a cold day in the pits o' 'ell before she ever married Malcolm Farnsworth. Said he was weak and greedy, but he'd do right by her when she told 'im the truth.'

There was another bellow of rage from the drawing room. Essie quickly eased the door open a crack.

'The girl went to her room. She didn't leave that night.' Everdene's heavy footsteps echoed through the house as he began to stomp up and down the room. 'She was a jezebel, but as a good Christian man, I would not throw her out in the cold of night,' he shouted.

Betsy winced in sympathy for her inspector and Constable Barnes. Their heads must be spinning by now. The man's voice was loud enough to wake the dead.

''Ere goes another one.' Essie hunched her thin shoulders and eased the door shut again. 'She was tossed out that night all right, right after the mistress slapped her.'

'Miss Everdene slapped Mary?' Betsy gave up all

pretence of trying to listen to what was going on in the drawing room. She'd finally decided she could only concentrate on one conversation at a time, and she was having much better luck getting the truth than the inspector was.

Essie grinned, her buck teeth making her look like a spiteful ferret. 'Oh yes, I 'eard the whole thing.' The girl's reedy voice dropped to an excited whisper. 'As soon as Miss Everdene got her drunken old father settled into the study, she come chargin' into the kitchen. But she were already too late.'

'Too late for what?'

'Too late to stop Mr Farnsworth. He'd already slipped me a note to give to Mary. He done it as soon as Miss Everdene were busy lookin' after 'er father. Ya see, she'd had the old fool propped up in the drawin' room, awaitin' for Mr Farnsworth to come in and ask for her 'and in marriage. But the reverend got restless and come out. He were weavin' all over the 'ouse when Mr Farnsworth got here. By that time, Mr Farnsworth had had plenty of time to slip me the note for Mary. He'd already gone into the study. He even used Miss Everdene's notepaper to write on.'

'So Miss Everdene didn't see Mr Farnsworth's note?' Betsy wanted to be sure she understood.

'Her? Nah, she didn't know nuthin' about that. She were just mad at the way Mary 'ad been all over Mr Farnsworth when Mary'd answered the door. Miss Everdene come chargin' into the kitchen like a mad dog huntin' a fox. She told the girl off right and proper for the way she'd been 'angin' onto Mr Farnsworth, but Mary weren't the least sorry. She'd already got what she wanted. Mr Farnsworth had noticed her. She just let Miss Everdene rant and rave for a few moments, and then she lifted her 'and and pointed to her finger. That's 'ow come I knows the mistress is in there lyin' to that peeler. She got a good gander at that ring.'

'Go on,' Betsy hissed. 'What happened then?'

'But I've already told ya.' Essie frowned. 'Mary jus' laughed and said Malcolm Farnsworth was no more goin' to be marryin' Miss Everdene than he was goin' to marry the Queen 'erself. Said that though he were a weak, greedy man, once Mary told him the truth about the baby, Malcolm would be marryin' 'er. Then she laughed again and rubbed her belly. That's when Miss Everdene 'it 'er. Slapped her right across the face and ordered 'er out o' the 'ouse.'

'Did Mary go?' Betsy couldn't believe her luck. She watched Essie's thin, plain face and excited eyes and wondered if the girl were telling the truth.

'She left all right, flounced right into our room, snatched up her carpetbag and waltzed out the front door with 'er nose in the air.'

Betsy cocked her ear towards the drawing room, just in case. 'And that was the last time you saw 'er?'

' 'Course not,' Essie said peevishly. 'I followed her out. This was the most excitin' thing that ever 'appened around 'ere. I didn't like to see Mary go. She weren't very nice, but she'd only been in the 'ouse a few hours and the fur was already flyin'. Besides, Mr Farnsworth give me a shillin' to deliver 'is note to her, and I were hopin' maybe Mary'd give me a bit as well.'

There was silence from the drawing room. 'How far did you follow her?' Betsy asked carefully. Essie's colourful speech patterns had made her very aware of her own tendency to lapse.

'Just to the corner. I could see she was 'eadin' for the 'igh Street. I started to call out to 'er, to say goodbye, but then I saw a feller step out of the trees on the other side of the road, so I turned around and come 'ome.'

'Was the man following Mary?' Betsy's heart began to beat faster.

Essie shrugged. 'I don't know. For a minute I thought it might be Mr Farnsworth – the bloke was dressed like a gent. But it weren't 'im. When I got back to the 'ouse, Mr Farnsworth was still here.'

'Did you read the note?' Betsy asked hopefully.

'Read!' Essie laughed incredulously. 'I can't read.'

'Well, did you listen in on Mr Farnsworth and Miss Everdene then?'

Essie gazed at her for a few moments before answering. 'I'm not rightly sure that I remember,' she said slyly.

'But just a moment ago, you remembered every little detail about that evening,' Betsy protested. Then she realized what the girl wanted. Obviously remembering that Malcolm Farnsworth had given her a shilling to deliver that note had reminded the girl that sometimes you could make a bit of money.

Sighing, Betsy reached into her cloak and pulled out some coins. Making sure she had enough for her fare home, she handed the rest over to Essie. She didn't begrudge the girl the money, for in truth Betsy could well remember what it was like to be poor and desperate.

Essie greedily snatched the coins. ' 'Course I listened in. Nothing else to do around 'ere, is there?'

'Did Miss Everdene mention anything about Mary Sparks to Mr Farnsworth?'

'Nah, she just talked sweet to 'im, pretended everything was fine. She didn't say a word about what 'appened in the kitchen. Stupid cow, 'e's only marryin' 'er fer 'er money.' Essie's lip curled up in a sneer. 'You'd think she'd figure that much out every time she looked in 'er mirror. Why would a 'andsome man like 'im want someone like 'er if'n she hadn't inherited a packet from her old grandmother?'

'So Miss Everdene inherited a rather large sum of money?' Betsy frowned thoughtfully.

Essie shook her head. 'Believe me, Mr Farnsworth couldn't see the woman for dust until 'e found out 'ow much she had. It's got the reverend's nose out of joint too. 'E'd been hopin' to keep Antonia at 'ome. But she put her foot down and said she was marryin' Malcolm Farnsworth whether 'e liked it or not. Two of 'em 'ad a right good row about it. But as she's the one that gets the money, she's the one that makes the rules now. She's of age. The old man can't keep 'er from marryin', and 'e knows it.'

'I don't care where that woman's body was found,' Everdene's voice boomed, 'it's nothing to do with us.'

Essie eased the door open again, and both women put their ears near the crack. Betsy heard the inspector say, 'But, sir, we're not insinuating it does have anything to do with either you or your daughter. I'm only asking if either of you knew the houses were sitting empty. After all, both of you are shareholders in Wildwoods. It's not inconceivable that the fact the houses were empty might have been mentioned here, and that

Miss Sparks overheard the remark and decided to take refuge there for the night.'

'She didn't leave here until the next morning,' Antonia Everdene insisted.

'Now she's lyin' again,' Essie said in disgust. 'Cor, acts so holy and then lies 'er bleedin' 'ead off to the coppers. Probably thinkin' by lyin' she's protectin' Malcolm Farnsworth.'

'Why would she need to do that? I thought you said he was still here after Mary left.' Betsy reluctantly pulled away from the door.

''E was, but 'e didn't stay long. 'E didn't even stay to eat, and he certainly didn't take Miss Everdene for a walk by the river like 'e did most times 'e come.' Essie smiled maliciously. ''E only stayed long enough to talk a bit, and then 'e claimed 'e had to get back to Knightsbridge. Said 'is friend's mother was feelin' poorly and 'e 'ad to get back to sit with her a spell.' She broke off and laughed. 'The only woman he were goin' to sit with was Mary Sparks. You could tell 'e couldn't wait to git out of 'ere and go to her.'

'So what time did he leave?'

Essie shrugged. 'Couldna been more than 'alf an 'our after 'e arrived. Miss Everdene was madder than a wet 'en. 'Ated to see all that fancy food she'd bought for the occasion wasted on her drunk of a father and 'erself. Right tight-fisted, she is. I wonder if she'll be so mean once she's married. Probably so, stingy is stingy if'n you ask me.'

Betsy gazed at the thin, plain girl and felt both pity and revulsion. Essie couldn't read or write, probably didn't have any parents and certainly didn't know the meaning of loyalty. But Betsy refused to judge her. There but for the grace of God go I, she thought humbly. If not for Inspector Witherspoon taking her in when she was sick, desperate and at her wit's end, she could well have ended up like this girl: illiterate, ignorant, ill-treated and ignored. Essie had been so hungry for someone to talk to that Betsy hadn't even had to come up with a reasonable story to get into the house and start asking questions.

'I expect you're leavin' now,' Essie said sadly.

'Yes, I'd better be goin'. They'll be getting worried if I don't get back soon.' She broke off and hesitated, wondering if she had the right to say what she couldn't suppress any longer.

'All right, then.' Essie squared her thin shoulders beneath the cheap fabric of her dress. 'I'll make sure there's no one 'angin' about, and you can slip out the back way.'

'Wait a minute.' Betsy couldn't help herself. There was something about this girl. 'Look, if you ever decide to leave here . . .'

'Leave 'ere? Where could I go? I'm not really trained. The only reason the Everdenes keep me on is because no one else will put up with 'em. They're 'orrible to work for, but at least it's a roof over me 'ead.' Essie gazed at her suspiciously. 'What are you on about?'

'Nothing,' Betsy said quickly. 'But if you ever do decide to leave here, come see me.' She started to offer to write Inspector Witherspoon's address down, but then she remembered that Essie couldn't read. 'You've a good memory, well, you must 'ave.' She quickly rattled off the address and then left before she could say anything more.

Witherspoon's ears ached by the time he and Constable Barnes were out of the Everdene house and safely into a hansom.

From out of his window the inspector spotted the figure of a heavily cloaked woman hurrying towards the High Street. Though he couldn't see the face, there was something very familiar about the way the woman moved.

'I'll wager that no one ever slept through one of his sermons,' Constable Barnes said with a groan. He rubbed his ears and winced.

'Only if they were deaf, Constable, only if they were deaf.' Witherspoon sighed and wished he could go home for a nice soothing cup of tea, but he couldn't. He still had to sort out this wretched murder case. And as if that weren't bad enough, his Chief Inspector was dropping hints that things weren't progressing fast enough to suit him. Well, really, the inspector thought, what do they expect me to do? It's not as though this were a simple case. Even identifying the victim had taken a dreadfully long time.

'We know that Mr Farnsworth is lying now,' Constable Barnes said in satisfaction. 'Wonder why he told us he didn't discover the ring were missing until he reached into his pocket to give it to Miss Everdene?'

'Perhaps, Constable, because it's true.'

'You mean you think the reverend's lyin'?' Barnes sounded scandalized.

'Well, we know that someone is, Constable,' Witherspoon said morosely. He didn't have a clue as to which of the prinicipals in this case wasn't telling the truth. But he was hardly going to admit that.

'Perhaps the Lutterbanks won't be as bad as this lot,' Barnes said hopefully as the hansom clip-clopped across the bridge.

'Hopefully,' the inspector muttered. 'But I highly doubt it. You know, Barnes, I never realized . . .'

'Realized what, sir?'

'That the rich were just as prone to lying as the poor.'

CHAPTER NINE

MRS JEFFRIES PAID the hansom driver and then paused to look around the busy corner. She glanced at the crumpled note in her hand and double-checked the address. Yes, this was the place where Wiggins had told her to meet him. Shepherd's Bush. Craning her neck, she stared across the heavy traffic on Goldhawk Road, to the Green, looking for the familiar face of their errant footman.

From behind, someone grabbed her elbow and spun her around, and she found herself face to face with a dishevelled Wiggins. 'Good gracious, Wiggins. You startled me. Now, where on earth have you been and what in heaven's name have you been up to?'

A smear of dirt was on his chin, his clothes were wrinkled, and there were dark circles under his eyes. 'Thank goodness you've come in time,' he gasped, ignoring her question. ''Urry. We've no time to lose. She'll be 'ere soon.' He tugged her round the corner onto Shepherd's Bush Road. 'Iwas scared she'd slip back into the 'ouse before you got a gander at 'er.'

'Just a moment,' Mrs Jeffries panted as the footman

pulled her around handcarts and dodged in and out of clusters of pedestrians. 'What are you talking about? Who are we looking for?'

''Urry,' he urged, ignoring her questions. 'She'll be 'ere any second.'

'Who?'

'There she is!' Wiggins said triumphantly as he pointed to a young woman crossing the road.

The girl was dressed in a pale lavender housedress covered by an apron. She was slender, blonde and very pretty. She wore a short cloak of brown wool over her dress and carried a large shopping basket.

They watched as she went into the grocer's shop.

'Is that who I think it is?' Mrs Jeffries asked.

'It's her, all right.'

She was so relieved. They weren't dealing with a madman! Cassie Yates had done precisely as she'd said she'd do. She'd got married. Wiggins pushed a lock of hair off his rather dirty forehead and nodded. But before he could explain further, Cassie came out of the shop and headed purposefully back the way she'd just come. The footman grabbed Mrs Jeffries's elbow again.

'Blimey,' he yelped. 'She's given the grocer her list. That means she'll be comin' back this afternoon to collect the basket. But we can't risk losin' her now. I think she knows she's bein' followed. She might 'ave spotted me yesterday.'

They dodged through the busy streets, keeping the brown cloak in sight. Mrs Jeffries was too winded to ask where they were going or how Wiggins had managed to find Cassie Yates so quickly. She was only glad that he had.

The chase ended at a tall brick house at the bottom of Dunsany Road. They had to duck behind a bush as the girl paused at the end of the small front garden and turned to have a quick, suspicious look around before she slipped into the house.

As soon as the door closed, Mrs Jeffries turned to the footman. 'Excellent, Wiggins, you've done a remarkable job. But the next time, do please let us know what you're up to. Despite that rather mysterious message from Mr Beaks, we've all been rather worried.'

Wiggins picked a blade of grass off his rumpled shirt. 'Sorry, Mrs Jeffries. But I were 'ot on the trail, and I 'ad to make sure she was the right one.' He brushed more dirt off his sleeve. 'Sorry about this too,' he mumbled, as the housekeeper glanced anxiously at his soiled clothes, 'but I've been sleepin' rough.'

'Oh dear, I do hope you won't take a chill.'

'Not to worry, I'm right as rain. Anyways, like I were sayin', it couldn't be helped.'

'However did you manage to find her?' Mrs Jeffries asked. 'Did she come back to Knightsbridge?'

'I found 'er by keepin' a sharp eye out on the McGraw 'ouse. Sure enough, once I'd figured out that Garrett's little nip of a brother come out to play the instant Garrett got 'ome every day, it were as plain as the nose on yer face,' Wiggins explained proudly. ''E were sending the lad to keep an eye on 'er. So instead of keepin' my eye on Garrett, I followed the little 'un, and he led me straight to 'er.'

Mrs Jeffries stared at the footman incredulously. 'Garrett McGraw's little brother? But what does that have to do with Cassie Yates?'

Now it was Wiggins's turn to look surprised. 'Cassie Yates? Who said anythin' about 'er? That girl that just went into that 'ouse in't Cassie Yates. She's Mary Sparks.'

Edgar Lutterbank glared at the inspector for a moment before shifting his hard gaze to Constable Barnes. 'I presume you've a good reason for this inconvenience?'

Inspector Witherspoon stifled a sigh. The Lutterbank family was being every bit as uncooperative as he'd feared. He and Constable Barnes had been kept waiting for half an hour before Mr Lutterbank would even condescend to see them.

'We're not trying to inconvenience you or your family.' Witherspoon smiled tightly at the four people staring at him with enmity. No, he corrected silently, only three of them were hostile. Mrs Lutterbank was pretending they weren't there. The pale, mousy woman had been gazing blankly at the wall since he and Constable Barnes had been shown into the drawing room.

'However,' he continued, trying to infuse some authority into his tone, 'this is a murder investigation. Mary Sparks was in your employ directly prior to her death. She spent less than twenty-four hours at the Everdene household. So if you don't mind, it would be most helpful if you can answer a few questions.'

'Of course we mind,' Edgar Lutterbank charged. 'But I don't see that we've any choice in the matter.' He pulled a watch out of his exquisitely tailored coat and frowned. 'But do get on with it, man, I've a meeting in the city in an hour.'

Witherspoon turned to Mrs Lutterbank. He might as well start with the least aggressive member of this household. 'As the mistress of the house,' he asked, 'could you explain your reasons for asking Mary Sparks to leave?'

Mrs Lutterbank ignored him. She continued to study the wallpaper.

'She didn't ask Mary to leave,' Mr Lutterbank cut in quickly. 'The girl left of her own accord and, I might add, without giving notice.'

Fiona Lutterbank, a plump, brown-haired girl who reminded Witherspoon of a pigeon, gave a short, high-pitched bark of laughter. It was not a pleasant sound.

'Oh, yes,' Fiona said as they all looked at her. 'Mary left without giving notice. Mama was so upset.'

The inspector suspected that might be a fabrication. He couldn't see that anything short of a blast of fireworks would upset Mrs Lutterbank. Why, the woman had barely blinked since he'd been there. 'But our information is that Miss Sparks left because she'd been let go.' The inspector addressed his question to Edgar Lutterbank. Out of the corner of his eye he saw Fiona turn her head sharply. He quickly shifted his gaze to the other side of the room and saw Fiona openly smirking at her brother, Andrew.

'Nonsense,' Mr Lutterbank snapped. 'I don't care what kind of ridiculous tales you've heard, it isn't true. Mary was a good worker. Why would we let her go? She just up and took it into her head to leave.'

'And you've no idea why?' the inspector asked.

'I think I know why,' Fiona said slyly. She giggled again. 'Mary must have overheard Mama and me talking about the Everdenes needing a parlour-maid. They're acquaintances of ours because Papa does business with them. I suppose the girl must have thought she wouldn't have to work so hard at a minister's house. Don't you think so, Andrew?'

Again she smirked at her brother. He gave her a tight smile, then looked at Witherspoon. Like his father, he was impeccably, if somewhat foppishly, dressed. He was a tall, thin man with a sharp aristocratic nose and weak chin. He smiled coolly at the inspector and said, 'I've really no idea. I don't make it a habit to concern myself with the servants' business.'

Despite his calm voice and the arrogant tilt to his head, Witherspoon had the impression Andrew Lutterbank was nervous. The chap was trying a bit too hard. His lazy posture seemed posed, his face too carefully blank. And the inspector had noticed that when the young man thought no one was looking, he nervously rubbed his chin.

'I'm sure you don't, Mr Lutterbank. But surely, you must have some idea why Miss Sparks would simply leave? According to witnesses, you were seen having a rather prolonged discussion with the girl on the day she left.' Witherspoon hoped he remembered that tidbit of gossip correctly, but he wasn't quite sure. Perhaps it had been someone else Andrew Lutterbank had been talking to that day. Drat, there were times when it was so difficult to keep facts straight in one's head.

'I don't care what you've been told,' Andrew said loudly. Too loudly. 'Mary was a servant here. If I was seen talking with her, it was probably because I wanted her to take better care in dusting my things. Except for giving her an occasional reprimand about shoddy work, I had nothing to do with her.'

Witherspoon noticed that he didn't deny he'd been speaking to the girl. 'Then why did you give her a brooch?'

Edgar Lutterbank leapt from his chair. 'Now, see here, Inspector.'

But Witherspoon ignored the outburst. He was too busy watching Andrew Lutterbank's face go utterly white. He had no idea if the young man had given Mary Sparks that brooch, but from his reaction, Witherspoon knew his shot in the dark had hit the target. His spirits soared. At last he was on the right track. Now perhaps they'd get somewhere in this case.

But the inspector's hopes were immediately dashed. For it wasn't Andrew Lutterbank who answered his question; it was his sister.

'Andrew didn't give Mary that brooch,' Fiona yelped. 'I gave it to her.'

'Really?' Witherspoon was terribly disappointed. 'Why?'

Fiona stared at him like a stricken rabbit. She swallowed convulsively. 'Because I felt sorry for her,' she mumbled.

'You felt sorry for the young lady?' The inspector had found that repeating an answer as a question often got results, and he was desperate enough to try anything.

Fiona's head bobbed up and down. 'Yes, her fiancé was away at sea, but he was due home in a couple of months. Mary didn't have anything nice, no trinkets or jewellery. She wanted to look pretty for Mark, and I didn't particularly like that old pin anyway, so I gave it to her.'

'Let me see now. You gave an expensive silver brooch to a servant because she didn't have any jewellery to wear for her sweetheart.' Inspector Witherspoon's brows rose. 'Is that what you're telling me?'

'My daughter speaks perfect English, Inspector,' Edgar Lutterbank said testily. 'If she says she gave the girl the trinket, then she did. Besides, what's this pin got to do with anything?'

'As the victim had the brooch pinned to her dress,' the inspector replied, 'we'd like to know precisely how a rather impoverished young woman went about acquiring it.' He turned back to Fiona. 'You didn't by any chance happen to give the girl a betrothal ring as well?'

Fiona blinked in surprise and shook her head. Mrs Lutterbank continued to stare at the wall, and Andrew slumped back against the settee.

'Really, Inspector.' Edgar Lutterbank's gaze narrowed suspiciously. 'Isn't that a rather ridiculous question? Come now, do ask something that makes sense. You're wasting all our time. Out of the kindness of her heart, my daughter gave the girl a trinket, and that's all. Why should any of us know anything about some betrothal ring?'

'The betrothal ring in question was purchased by a Mr Malcolm Farnsworth to give to his fiancée,' Witherspoon explained. 'The gentleman is, I believe, acquainted with the family.'

'Certainly. Both young Malcolm and Emery Clements are frequently guests of my son. But I assure you, sir, we're not in the habit of relieving them of their valuables and passing them on to the servants.'

'I certainly didn't mean to imply any such thing.' The inspector wasn't sure what he had meant to imply, but he did think this line of questioning was producing some interesting results. He glanced at Constable Barnes and found the man gazing at him in admiration. 'So you've no idea how Mary Sparks happened to be wearing an expensive betrothal ring when she was murdered?' He slowly turned his head, gazing expectantly at the four Lutterbanks.

'I believe I can solve that particular mystery,' Andrew Lutterbank drawled. 'Malcolm happened to lose the ring the very day he bought it. We'd been out in the gardens having tea. Mary obviously found it and picked it up.'

Inspector Witherspoon deliberately kept his expression blank. How on earth did Andrew Lutterbank know the ring had been lost when Malcolm Farnsworth didn't? But he wasn't going to show his hand now. Oh no, the inspector thought craftily. Before he pursued any more questions about that ring he'd have another word with Mr Farnsworth. Nodding to the young man, he turned to Edgar Lutterbank. 'Are you a shareholder in Wildwoods?'

One of Mr Lutterbank's heavy grey eyebrows rose. 'Yes. Not that it's any business of the Metropolitan Police.'

Witherspoon looked at Fiona and quickly asked, 'Other than her fiancé, was Mary Sparks seeing any other men?'

Fiona's mouth gaped in surprise for a split second before she recovered. 'Well, yes,' she said, giving the inspector a knowing smile. 'Actually, Mary was a flirt.

181

I believe there were several young men who were smitten with her. And she encouraged them all.'

Mrs Lutterbank suddenly straightened. 'Oh yes,' she chirped brightly. 'Oh yes, there were always men. She was a tart. Men all the time. Why in this very house, I've had to speak harshly . . .'

As Mrs Lutterbank rambled on about harlots and tarts, Edgar Lutterbank's face darkened to crimson. Suddenly he leapt to his feet. 'That's enough,' he roared, and Mrs Lutterbank jumped and ceased her muttering. He turned to the inspector. 'My wife's not well, sir. These questions have upset her terribly. Fiona, take your mother to her room.'

A swell of sympathy filled Witherspoon as he watched Fiona lead the poor woman away. He realized now that the reason she'd been sitting quietly and staring at the wall was probably that she was a tad touched in the head. Really, it was such a shame.

He waited until the two women had gone and then turned to Mr Lutterbank. 'About Wildwoods, sir. I'm afraid your association with that company is very much the business of the police. Mary Sparks's body was discovered in one of Wildwoods's properties.' He looked quickly at Andrew. 'Would you mind telling me, sir, where you were on the night of September the tenth?'

Edgar Lutterbank quickly stepped between the inspector and his son, blocking the policeman's view of Andrew's expression.

'He was at home,' Edgar supplied hastily.

Witherspoon studied the older man for a moment. 'You must have a remarkable memory, sir.'

'Not at all, Inspector.' Lutterbank retorted. 'I don't

need a remarkable memory to know where my son was on that particular evening. He was at home every evening in September.'

'Surely that's unusual.' Witherspoon tilted his head to one side and tried to give Andrew a disbelieving smile. 'A wealthy bachelor spending all of his free time at home . . .' He let his voice trail off meaningfully.

'There's nothing in the least peculiar about my staying home,' Andrew said, getting up from the settee and coming to stand beside his father. 'My mother wasn't well in September. I wanted to be close by in case she took a turn for the worse.'

'I see.' The inspector tried to think of something else to ask. Unfortunately, nothing occurred to him. 'Well, if you can think of anything else which might shed some light on this matter,' he said, 'do please contact me at the Yard. I take it none of you have any plans to leave London? We may need to ask a few more questions.'

'Now, see here, Inspector,' Edgar Lutterbank protested. 'Don't you think you're being unreasonable? Are you telling us we can't leave the city?'

'No, no, of course not,' Witherspoon answered.

'Well it's a jolly good thing. Not leave London, indeed!' Lutterbank snorted. 'I'm going to the continent in a few days, and I'm taking my son with me. Business trip. Now, if you've an objection to that, perhaps I'll have a word with your superiors.'

'That won't be necessary,' the inspector replied wearily. 'You're free to go where you please.'

He signalled to Constable Barnes to put away his notebook and took his leave of the Lutterbank family.

He couldn't wait to get home and have a nice, quiet cup of tea. Thank goodness this tiresome day was almost over.

Mrs Jeffries listened carefully to the details of Inspector Witherspoon's day. She clucked her tongue sympathetically, ladled more potatoes onto his plate and gently asked a few questions. Tense herself because of what she and the others would be doing later, she barely listened as he repeated the facts of the interview he'd had with the Everdenes. Mrs Jeffries wasn't worried overmuch by missing any of that tale – she'd already heard the entire story from Betsy.

'I believe I'll turn in early, Mrs Jeffries,' Witherspoon announced as he pushed his plate aside and stood up. 'Perhaps a good night's sleep will help rid me of this dreadful headache.'

She quickly assured him that that was precisely what he needed. As soon as he disappeared up the stairs, she hurried to the hall closet, grabbed her hat and cloak and raced to the kitchen.

Betsy and Mrs Goodge were waiting at the kitchen table.

'Smythe should be back any minute now,' the maid told her. 'He'll have had time to get to Luty's and back.'

'Good. Did Smythe have time to tell you what he'd learned today?' She looked expectantly at the two women. They both shook their heads.

'He only had time to snatch a bite to eat,' Mrs Goodge explained. 'Before he left to get the carriage and Luty Belle.'

As they waited for the coachman to return, she told

them everything she'd learned from the inspector over dinner. 'We must be sure and tell Smythe everything too,' she finished, cocking her head towards the street as her sharp ears picked up the distinctive sound of a carriage turning the corner.

'I'll ride up front with 'im and let 'im know,' Betsy volunteered eagerly. As the coach drew up out front, she picked up her cloak. 'Hope the inspector stays abed tonight. Wouldn't look right for 'im to ring for something and find us all gone.'

'Not to worry,' Mrs Goodge said calmly. 'I can hear his bell from me room. I'll take care of the dining room too. Give me somethin' to do while I'm waiting for you to get back. If'n the inspector wants something, I can fetch it. Besides, all I have to do is 'int that you and Mrs J are feelin' poorly, and he wouldn't think of askin' where you be. He'll think you're abed.'

'Thank you, Mrs Goodge,' Mrs Jeffries said to the cook. 'I don't know how we'd manage without you. We don't like leaving you to cope, but it's vitally important we confront Mary Sparks.'

By the time they arrived outside the brick house on Dunsany Road, Luty Belle was quivering with excitement. 'I still can't understand why Mary didn't come to me,' she said, pulling her bright purple cloak tighter against the cool chill of the night.

'Yes, that's very curious, isn't it?' Mrs Jeffries reached for the door latch as soon as the horses stopped. 'And that's why we want you with us when we talk to her. I've a feeling that whatever it is she's hiding, she'll be more apt to tell the truth if you're there.'

'Stop frettin', Hepzibah,' Luty ordered as she nimbly leapt from the carriage. 'Mary will tell the truth.'

'It's about time you got 'ere,' Wiggins whispered. He'd come from his hiding place in the bushes when he'd seen the coach round the corner.

'Is she still there?' Mrs Jeffries asked.

'Yeah. No one's gone in or out since the last lodger got home at half past six.'

'Come on.' Luty headed for the house. 'Let's git this over with.'

With Luty Belle in the lead, they marched up the walkway and banged the knocker. A moment later the door opened and a tall middle-aged woman with black hair peered out.

'Yes, what is it?' she asked sharply. 'I've no rooms to let now—' She broke off as she became aware of the small crowd littering her stoop. 'Here now, what's all this? What do you lot want?'

Luty Belle stepped forward. 'We've come to see Mary Sparks. We knows she's here, and we're not leavin' until we see her.'

The woman looked taken aback for an instant, and then her bony face hardened. Mrs Jeffries quickly shoved Luty to one side.

'Please forgive my friend's rather bold manner,' she began pleasantly. She ignored Luty's snort of derision. 'But it's terribly important that we speak to Mary Sparks. One could almost say it was a matter of life and death. This is Mrs Luty Belle Crookshank, and she's a dear friend of Mary's. We've been so very worried about the girl. We must see her.'

The woman regarded her suspiciously for a moment

and then stepped back and opened the door wider. 'I'm Agnes Finch. Go on through to the parlour. I'll see if Mary wants to see you.'

They trooped into the parlour, and a few moments later Mary Sparks appeared. Puzzled, she stopped in the doorway and gazed at the unfamiliar faces. When she reached Luty Belle's, she gasped and rushed forward. 'Oh, Mrs Crookshank, it's you. I'm so glad you've come.'

'Well, I reckon I had to come,' Luty exclaimed as she rose and gave the girl a hug. 'You weren't exactly bustin' your horses to come see me, was ya?'

'I'm so sorry,' Mary pleaded. She bit her lower lip. 'But I've been so scared. Everythin's so mixed up. Garrett said I should just wait here until Mark come home before I did anything.' She paused and cast a quick, curious glance at the others.

'These are my friends,' Luty hastily explained. 'If'n you didn't murder Cassie Yates, then they've come to help.'

Mary's eyes widened, and she paled. 'Then she really is dead. I knew somethin' had happened to her,' she whispered.

'You knew Cassie had been murdered?' Mrs Jeffries interjected softly.

'No.' Mary shook her head. 'I mean, I thought somethin' bad might have happened to her, but I didn't know it were murder.'

'Why'd ya think somethin' had happened to Cassie?' Luty asked. 'Dang and blast, this ain't makin' no sense at all. How'd you come to get mixed up with Cassie Yates and her troubles?'

'I didn't want to get mixed up with her,' Mary said

earnestly. 'But I didn't have no choice about it. Then, after she didn't show up to collect her pouch, I knew somethin' was wrong.'

Luty's gaze sharpened. 'What pouch?'

'The one she gave me to keep for her . . .'

Mrs Jeffries stepped forward again. 'I think it would be best if Mary sat down and told us what happened in her own good time.'

Mary looked at Luty for guidance, and when the elderly woman nodded, she sat down on the settee.

Betsy and Smythe leaned forward, Wiggins balanced on the edge of his chair and even Mrs Jeffries was excited. She forced herself to calm down. 'Now,' she said, sitting down across from Mary and Luty Belle. 'Why don't you tell us what happened?'

The girl chewed her lower lip and twisted her hands together in her lap. 'I'm not right sure where to begin.'

'Why don't you start with the event that led you to decide to leave the Lutterbank house?' Mrs Jeffries suggested smoothly.

Mary nodded. 'Well, it were the day before I went to Mrs Crookshank. I were upstairs dusting the landin' when all of a sudden, Andrew Lutterbank slinks up behind me and tried to put his arms around me waist.' She wrinkled her nose in disgust. 'He's done that before, but this time it were different.'

'Different how?' Mrs Jeffries asked.

'Bolder. Like he didn't care if I said somethin' to his father. I slapped his hands and told him to leave me be, but he just laughed and lunged at me again. This time I stepped back far enough to run if I had to, and that made him stop. I told him if he didn't leave me be, I'd tell his father, and he just laughed and said he didn't care.' Mary shook her head. 'Said he didn't need to worry any more, that he had a bit of money comin' to him. But I knew that were a lie. He'd been lickin' his father's boots for weeks tryin' to get Mr Lutterbank to give him back his allowance. Andrew hadn't had as much as a farthing from Mr Lutterbank since he got Sally Comstock in the family way, and they used Andrew's allowance to pay her off and ship her to Australia.'

'So you know about that,' Mrs Jeffries said. She remembered that Mary wasn't at the Lutterbank house when that incident had occurred. 'Who told you?'

'Cassie told me,' Mary replied. 'But it weren't a secret. Everyone in the house knew what had happened. Oh yes, everyone knows. Especially with Cassie goin' on about it all the time. You'd have had to been deaf as a post not to have heard the story.'

'Then what happened?' Luty asked impatiently.

'Well, after I told him to leave me be, he flounced out of the house and into the garden. Mr Farnsworth and Mr Clements were waitin' for him. I watched from the window. I didn't want to run into him, and I were hopin' he'd be goin' out with the other gentlemen. They often went to their club and played cards – gamblin' and the like.'

'But how could Andrew gamble?' Mrs Jeffries asked. 'You said he didn't have any money.' She frowned as she remembered the gossip Mrs Goodge had told her.

'He didn't use money. Least he hadn't been. He used the belongin's he had in his room,' Mary explained. 'He had a lot of nice things some old relative who'd died out in India had left him. Strange kinds of objects, gold candlesticks, jewels, a pair of ivory-handled daggers. His friends were quite willing to let him play with that instead of money. He'd already lost most of them because Sarah, the upstairs maid, weren't complainin' so much about how long it took her to dust.'

'All right, so we know that Lutterbank had a yen to gamble every now and agin,' Luty said impatiently. 'But time's awastin'. Git on with the story, girl. What happened next?'

'Well, after he went into the garden, I decided I had to leave. It were one thing to stay when Andrew was behavin' himself, but after what he'd just told me about not carin' what his father thought no more and not needin' his allowance, I knew I'd best get out and find myself another position.' Mary paused and took a deep breath. 'There was somethin' not right goin' on in that house. Somethin' I couldn't quite put my finger on, and I just wanted to go. I'd heard about another position, over in Putney, at a minister's house.'

'Who told you about the position?' It was Betsy who asked that question.

'Cassie Yates. Miss Fiona had sent me out that day to get her a box of chocolates. I met Cassie when she was comin' out the side gate of the garden.'

'Who'd Cassie been visiting?' Betsy interrupted.

'I don't know. I never asked,' Mary admitted. 'But anyways, she saw that I were upset and asked me what was wrong. I told her I'd decided to leave, and she told me about the Everdenes needin' a new maid. She give me the name of the domestic agency that was doin' the hirin' as well.'

'Did Cassie ask you why you wanted to leave?' Mrs Jeffries asked.

'No, she didn't have to. I think she knew.' Mary made a wry face. 'Not that she were ever scared of Andrew; she weren't. But that's neither here nor there. Early the next mornin' I give Fiona Lutterbank the news that I were leavin' and I wouldn't be back. Then I went to Mrs Crookshank.'

'Why'd ya lie to me about that brooch?' Luty asked sharply.

'But I didn't.' Mary turned earnest eyes to her friend. 'You see, when I told Miss Lutterbank I were leavin' she accused me of stealin' her silver brooch. But I never took no brooch. I never took nothin' from her. So I told her she were wrong and I left.'

Luty stared at the girl's pleading face for a few seconds and then grinned. 'Reckon you're tellin' the truth, child.' She reached over and patted Mary's hand. 'Git on with your tale.'

Relieved, Mary nodded. 'Mrs Crookshank wrote me a letter of reference and let me spend the night. The next day, I put on my best dress and went to the domestic agency that hired for the Everdenes. I got the job. They told me to get over to Putney as soon as I could. I went back and said goodbye to Mrs Crookshank, picked up my carpetbag and started for the Everdene house. On my way I happened to pass by the shop where Cassie Yates used to be employed. Well, she'd already give that position up, so I were right surprised when I heard her calling me to stop.' Mary swallowed and dropped her gaze to her lap. 'I didn't want to, but she said she had to talk to me, said it were important. We went to her rooms, and then she started askin' me a lot o' questions.'

'What kind of questions?' Mrs Jeffries interjected.

'She started off by askin' if I'd got the job and had anyone from the Everdene house seen me. I told her I was to start that day and that the only person I'd seen except for the lady that did the interviewin' was a well-dressed woman who come into the office just as I were leavin'.' Mary broke off and shuddered. 'I didn't know it then, but she had somethin' in mind with all them questions. Before I could say Bob's-your-uncle, she ordered me to change clothes with her.'

'Change clothes with her?' Wiggins looked positively scandalized.

'Yes. Then she told me I weren't goin' to be workin' for the Everdenes; she was. She were goin' to pretend she were me and take the post.'

'Why did you go along with this?' Luty asked indignantly.

'I didn't have no choice,' Mary explained. 'When I tried to tell her I wouldn't do it, she pulled that silver brooch out of her reticule and dangled it under me nose; then she reached into her pocket and pulled out a handful of pound notes. She said she'd taken the money and pin from Fiona Lutterbank, and she'd done it wearin' my old grey cloak. She said she'd made sure several people saw her leavin' the house wearin' my cloak. If I didn't do as she asked, she'd tell the Lutterbanks where I was goin' and they'd have me put in jail.' Her voice trembled, and she broke off for a moment and turned to Luty Belle. 'You were already gone to Venice, Mark was still at sea and I didn't know what to do. I changed clothes with her and she left.'

'You poor girl,' Wiggins murmured. 'All alone and frightened. It's a cryin' shame, that's what it is . . .'

'Wiggins, please,' Mrs Jeffries said. 'Go on, Mary. What did you do then?'

'Well, I waited until it were evening and I went back to Knightsbridge. I were hopin' that Garrett could help me. But he couldn't do anythin' until the next day. He couldn't take me home with him – there's not a spare bed at their house, and he couldn't bring me here because Mrs Finch weren't home. So he told me to go to Magpie Lane. He said he overheard Mr Clements tell Mr Andrew and Mr Farnsworth about the houses bein' empty. Garrett said for me to go to the back of one of the houses and break a window. Said the whole street were deserted and no one would hear. So we waited a bit, and then I got a hansom and left.'

'Why did you delay going to Magpie Lane?' Mrs Jeffries asked.

'I didn't want Mr Andrew to see me on the street. Garrett and I had to hide in some bushes until Mr Andrew got his own hansom and went off. It took a bit of time. Hansoms were hard to come by that night. It were pouring with rain.'

'When you were there that night, did you hear any other cabs go up the road?'

Mary nodded. 'Oh yes. For a deserted street it had a bit of traffic that evening. I were trying to sleep when I heard the first one, then right after that the second one, and then, a good hour later, the third cab come around the corner. After midnight, I was able to finally doze off.'

'When did you realize that Cassie Yates was missing?' Mrs Jeffries asked softly. She watched Mary's face closely, but the girl continued to gaze at her openly.

'The next day,' she replied in low voice. 'I knew something was badly wrong the next day. Cassie had told me to meet her at a tea shop, but she never showed. I knew something had happened then.'

Betsy leaned forward. 'What made you so certain?'

'Because Cassie had given me a pouch for safe-keepin'. I was to bring it to her the next day. But she never came.'

'What was in the pouch?' Mrs Jeffries asked.

Mary bit her lip again, and her eyes flooded with tears. 'Money. Lots of it.'

CHAPTER TEN

Mrs Jeffries ignored the gasps from the other occupants of the room. 'Money,' she repeated softly. 'Are you sure?'

Mary brushed at her cheeks. 'I'm sure. It liked to frighten me to death, walkin' about London with a pouch full of pound notes.'

'How much money are we talkin' 'ere?' Smythe asked.

Mary turned to look at him and shrugged her shoulders. 'Well, I didn't count it, so I don't rightly know. But it were a lot, more than I've ever seen before.'

'When Cassie didn't show up,' Mrs Jeffries asked softly, 'what did you do with the pouch?'

'I took it to Knightsbridge,' Mary replied, giving Luty Belle an anxious glance. 'I hid it in one of them tubs on Mrs Crookshank's terrace.'

'One of my tubs,' Luty repeated. 'You mean one of them big fancy urns I've been plantin' my orange trees in?'

'Yes. Garrett had told me he'd dug them out that day,' Mary explained hastily. 'And I couldn't think of any other place where the money would be safe. You know, in case Cassie showed up and wanted it back. So when I went to the gardens that day, I waited till there was no one around, then I shoved the pouch in the bottom o' the tub and piled a bit o' dirt on top to hide it. I didn't know what else to do,' she wailed. 'I couldn't even tell Garrett about the money. I didn't want him involved any more than he was. But I didn't want to keep it. Cassie's money didn't belong to me! I weren't rightly sure that money even belonged to her. I don't know how she got it, but when she didn't show up, I knew I didn't want to hang on to it.'

Mrs Jeffries tilted her head to one side and studied the girl's earnest expression. 'Why did you feel so strongly about it? Cassie had blackmailed you out of a position, and you hadn't much money of your own. Under those circumstances, I should think you'd have been very tempted to hang on to that pouch.'

'Tempted to steal?' Mary cried. 'I'm no thief, Mrs Jeffries, and it's a right good thing too. I reckon Cassie were murdered for that money. If I'd a kept it, the same thing would have happened to me.'

'Why do you think the money caused Cassie's murder?' Luty Belle asked bluntly. 'Are you sayin' you know who wanted the money, you know who wanted her dead?'

Mary hesitated. 'I'm not sure. But I know she didn't come by that money honestly. She had ways of gettin' things from people, usually men. And I know that she was plannin' on causin' a lot of trouble, and I didn't want any part o' it.'

Luty's black eyes narrowed. 'Trouble fer who?'

'Malcolm Farnsworth, for one,' Mary replied. 'I knew about him because she told me when we was a-changin' clothes so she could take my place at the Everdene house. She went on and on about him, almost like she didn't know what she were sayin'. She said she wasn't lettin' him get away with it, that he'd do right by her if it was the last thing he ever did, and that if he thought payin' her off with a few quid would get rid of her, he had another think comin'.'

'Cor,' Smythe exclaimed. 'She said all that?' He looked at Mrs Jeffries. 'It wouldn't be the first time a man's done killin' to keep his secrets from showin'. Looks to me like we might 'ave a motive for murder 'ere.'

'So it would appear.' Mrs Jeffries turned to Mary. 'Did Cassie say what she planned to do when she got to the Everdene house?'

'No, she just rambled on about how Malcolm would see that she didn't mean to be trifled with. That he'd have to marry her or she'd cause a scandal.' Mary shrugged. 'When I asked her how she could do that, she told me that if she had to, she'd stand right up in church if Malcolm tried to marry Antonia Everdene. Said she'd tell the whole world she was going to have Malcolm's bastard.' Mary broke off as a blush crept up her cheeks. 'It weren't very nice language, I know. But that's what she said.'

Betsy pursed her lips. 'So you're sayin' that Cassie went to the Everdenes' just to show Malcolm he couldn't get rid of her?'

'That's what she said,' Mary answered. 'But I thought she was talkin' crazy. She'd already taken money from him.'

'You mean she claimed the money in the pouch was definitely from Malcolm Farnsworth?' Mrs Jeffries felt this was an important point.

'Well, she didn't exactly say he give her the money,' Mary admitted, 'but who else was there? And I know she saw Malcolm that day, 'cause she showed me a ring he give her. It were a pretty one too. She had it on a chain round her neck.'

'But if'n he give Cassie a ring,' Wiggins put in, confused, 'wouldn't that mean he meant to marry 'er?'

Betsy snorted. 'Not always. If Cassie were raisin' a fuss, he might 'ave given her the ring to keep her quiet. He probably lied through his teeth and told Cassie he'd marry her. Then, when she found out he were really fixin' to propose to Antonia Everdene, she might have been mad enough to want to get a bit of her own back.'

'But 'ow would Cassie know that Malcolm Farnsworth was goin' to ask Miss Everdene for her 'and?' Wiggins asked curiously.

It was Mary who answered. 'She could have found out easy enough. Cassie was always hangin' about . . . She might have seen Andrew Lutterbank that day, and he might have told her. Like I said before, Cassie weren't scared of Mr Andrew. She used to brag that she knew how to handle him. She were half-mad that day, rantin' and ravin' about Malcolm and Emery Clements and Andrew Lutterbank. She might have seen any of them, and any of them could have told her about Malcolm plannin' on proposin' to Miss Everdene.'

'Did she specifically state she'd seen any of those gentlemen?' Mrs Jeffries asked. She watched the girl carefully.

'Not exactly,' Mary replied slowly. 'I don't recall evrythin' she said that mornin', but I do remember I had a . . . a . . .'

'Impression,' Betsy supplied helpfully.

'That's right, a impression she'd seen them all. But I couldn't say for certain.' Mary sighed. 'All I know is I was ever so glad when she left and I could get away.'

'So the last time you saw Cassie Yates was the morning she made you change clothes and took your place at the Everdene house, is that correct?' Mrs Jeffries asked briskly.

'That's right.'

'Why have you been hiding yurself?' Luty asked. She tilted her chin and stared hard at the girl.

Mrs Jeffries saw Mary's throat muscles move as the girl swallowed. Finally, she said, 'Because I was scared of Malcolm. Garrett told me that no one had seen Cassie about since that day she went to the Everdenes'. Malcolm was still engaged to Antonia Everdene, and I knew Cassie wouldn't have stood for that. I knew somethin' bad must have happened, but I didn't have no real proof that he'd done anythin'. What could I say? Who'd believe me? I didn't even know for sure she was dead until tonight.'

'But didn't you see the story of the body being discovered in the newspapers?' Mrs Jeffries asked.

Mary shook her head. 'No, I don't have money to waste on newspapers. I knew I should do somethin' about Cassie, but I weren't sure what. So I decided to stay here until Mark come back. He'd know the best thing to do.'

Mrs Jeffries nodded and asked, 'And when is your fiancé due back?'

'At the end of the week,' Mary replied with a shy smile.

'Good,' Luty said firmly. 'But afore then, you'd best come with me to see Inspector Witherspoon. We'll go tomorrow morning. Cassie Yates mightn't a been much good, but she didn't deserve to be murdered and stashed in some dark hole of a cellar like she was nothin'.'

'You want me to go to the police?' Mary's voice squeaked in alarm.

'But of course, my dear,' Mrs Jeffries said firmly. 'You must tell Inspector Witherspoon everything you've told us.'

'But what about Mr Malcolm? I don't want him comin' after me.'

'You needn't fear Malcolm Farnsworth,' Mrs Jeffries said soothingly. 'I'm sure that once the inspector hears what you have to say, Mr Farnsworth will no longer be a problem.'

As soon as she said the words, something tugged at the back of her mind. She tried to grasp what it was, but she couldn't.

'Don't you worry none,' Luty said as she stamped her cane. 'You jus' go pack yer things and come with me. You can stay at my house till yer man gets back, and don't be frettin' none about a no-good polecat like Farnsworth. I keep a six-shooter under my bed, and Hatchet's purty danged good with a rifle. We ain't scared a him. Tomorrow mornin' we'll go see the inspector, and by tomorrow night Mr Malcolm

Murderin' Farnsworth will be locked up tighter than the crown jewels.'

Inspector Witherspoon allowed himself a smug smile as Mrs Jeffries took his hat and coat. He couldn't help it. For once, the day had gone exceedingly well. Perfectly, in fact. This wretched murder was virtually solved. By tomorrow morning, they'd have the rest of the evidence they needed to arrest the murderer.

'You're looking very happy, sir,' Mrs Jeffries said as she hung his hat on the rack and then turned and led the way to the drawing room. 'Have you had a good day?'

'An excellent day, Mrs Jeffries,' the inspector said as he settled into his favourite chair. 'We've made monumental progress in this case. Why, it's practically solved. I must say, your comments this morning at breakfast helped enormously. You were quite right, you know. The only way to truly determine if Antonia Everdene was telling the truth was to question her servants.' He broke off and accepted a glass of sherry. 'I must say, we had a spot of luck there.' He broke off and frowned slightly. 'Er, I hope you don't mind, but when it became clear that Essie Tuttle wouldn't tell us the truth because she was afraid of losing her position, I did make a rather, a well . . . a rash promise.'

'Oh?'

'Yes, I'm afraid I had to assure the girl that I'd find her another post,' Witherspoon confessed. 'Well, I thought that if the worst came to the worst, perhaps you could find a spot for her here. I know you're in charge of the household, Mrs Jeffries, and I certainly wouldn't be presumptuous enough to interfere in any way, but do you possibly think we could find something for Essie to do here at Upper Edmonton Gardens?' He leaned forward, his expression earnest. 'I know that's not a particularly usual method of getting the truth from a witness, but honestly, Mrs Jeffries, the poor girl was utterly terrified. I couldn't get a word out of her until I'd told her I'd find her another place. If you don't think she'd fit in here, do you suppose Mrs Crookshank might be able to use another housemaid? Her house is rather enormous, and despite dear Mrs Crookshank being rather eccentric, she strikes one as being a most kindhearted soul.'

'Not to worry, sir,' Mrs Jeffries said quickly, wanting to get the inspector back to the case. 'I'm sure that between Luty and me we can work something out for the girl. Now, do go on, sir. I'm burning with curiosity.'

The inspector sighed with relief. 'Oh, gracious,' he cried, 'I'm forgetting to give you the best news of all.'

Mrs Jeffries prepared to look surprised.

'Luty Belle came to see me this morning, and you'll never guess who she brought with her.'

'Who?'

'Mary Sparks.' Witherspoon answered smugly. 'She isn't dead. The body we found in Magpie Lane is Cassie Yates.'

'Goodness, really?'

For the next ten minutes, Witherspoon related how Luty Belle Crookshank had shown up at the Yard with Mary Sparks in tow. He repeated Mary's story almost verbatim. 'Of course,' he concluded, 'we realized Miss Sparks must be telling the truth when we accompanied them back to Mrs Crookshank's and dug up that pouch. It had over five hundred pounds inside!'

'Goodness, that's a lot of money.' There was another faint tug at the back of Mrs Jeffries's mind. But it disappeared as quickly as it had come.

'It was a piece of luck that I'd already decided to go to the Everdene house again,' the inspector continued happily. 'Hearing Mary's story gave us precisely the information we needed to ask the right questions.'

'Nonsense, Inspector,' Mrs Jeffries said briskly. 'Luck had nothing to do with it. As usual, you're being far too modest. It was your own brilliant detective work that made you realize that the Everdenes were trying to hide something. You've an instinct for such things, sir. Tell me,' she continued when he beamed with pleasure, 'what did Mr Farnsworth say when you confronted him this afternoon?'

'At first he tried to deny everything,' Witherspoon said. 'But when the chap realized that we had a witness to the fact that he'd left the Everdene house shortly after Cassie Yates did, and that we knew all about his relationship with her, he caved in and admitted the truth.'

'He admitted he killed her?' Mrs Jeffries asked in astonishment.

'Oh no, no. He admitted they'd been . . .' he broke off, blushed a deep pink and lowered his eyes to his glass, 'intimate. He also admitted he'd seen her earlier that day and told her it was all over between them. He gave her fifty pounds.'

'Did he give her anything else, sir?' She hoped the inspector had discovered how Cassie Yates had ended up with Antonia Everdene's betrothal ring around her neck.

'No, just the money. Mind you, he claimed not to know anything about the five hundred pounds we'd found in that pouch. Claimed he didn't have any idea where that had come from.'

Mrs Jeffries thought that was odd. Why would he lie about how much he'd given Cassie to get out of his life? 'That's a silly thing to lie about.'

'Yes, I thought so too,' the inspector agreed. 'Mind you, Farnsworth claims that once he gave Cassie the fifty pounds, she agreed to let him alone. But obviously she changed her mind and threatened to tell Miss Everdene about the child. Farnsworth killed her to make sure his marriage to an heiress wasn't in jeopardy.'

'How did she get the betrothal ring?' she asked.

Witherspoon raised his eyebrows. 'Farnsworth claims she stole it from him on the morning he asked Miss Everdene to marry him. That's probably how Cassie realized Farnsworth was going to wed Miss Everdene. She saw the betrothal ring. He admits he saw her that day before he went to the Lutterbanks. That's how he met Cassie, you know. They began their association when she was still working there.' He sighed. 'Poor silly woman, if she'd stayed away from that greedy monster, she'd still be alive. Sad, isn't it? There's so very much tragedy about.'

Mrs Jeffries didn't want the inspector to get started on one of his philosophical discourses. Frequently they had a number of quite interesting chats about the world, the cosmos and the nature of life, but this evening she needed information.

'Of course there is, sir,' she said quickly. 'But you and men like yourself are certainly doing your very best to make the world a better place. Speaking of which, did Mr Farnsworth say what happened when he arrived at Magpie Lane?'

'He did indeed.' Witherspoon clucked his tongue. 'I say, I do so hate it when people lie. The man actually expected us to believe that when he got there, the house was empty. He said there wasn't hide nor hair of Cassie Yates anywhere. Naturally, he claimed he never looked in the cellar, said he didn't even know the house had a cellar. Well, he'd hardly admit he dragged her down there and stabbed her, would he?'

'Certainly not. Have you found the weapon yet?'

'Not yet, but we will. We've started looking for the hansom drivers that took him to and from Magpie Lane. Oh, by the way, Farnsworth confessed that he and Cassie had been meeting secretly there for weeks. That's why he told her to meet him there in the note.'

'Yes, sir,' Mrs Jeffries agreed. 'Now, you were saying?'

The inspector gave her a blank look.

'We were talking about the murder weapon,' she reminded him.

'Of course, of course. What I was getting at is now that we know they were meeting in Magpie Lane, we'll start looking for witnesses. There'll be the hansom driver from that night and, I daresay, many others. If we get really lucky, we may even find someone who saw Mr Farnsworth tossing something in the River Thames.'

Mrs Jeffries felt the inspector would hardly be that lucky, but she didn't like to say so.

'I wanted to search his rooms today,' Witherspoon

continued, 'but Mr Clements raised such a fuss I decided it would be better to wait until after we'd made an arrest.'

'Emery Clements didn't want you to search Mr Farnsworth's rooms? Why ever not?' Mrs Jeffries thought of all the gossip she'd heard about Cassie. The girl hadn't been involved only with Malcolm Farnsworth and Andrew Lutterbank. She'd also been seeing Clements. Then she caught herself. This case was solved. There was no need for her to keep prying about for additional suspects.

'He kept muttering about us being on a fishing expedition and not bringing a warrant. Said that as we weren't actually arresting Mr Farnsworth right then, we'd no right to search his home. Sent for his solicitor. But don't worry, Mrs Jeffries.' Witherspoon set his empty glass down on the table. 'I've got several men watching the Clements's house. They'll make sure nothing is taken out of the place before I get a chance to have a good look round. We'll have both a warrant and an arrest by tomorrow morning.'

'Are you going to ask Cassie's landlady to try and identify Mr Farnsworth?'

'Well, er, no.' Witherspoon stared at her in surprise. 'Farnsworth admitted he and Cassie used to meet in Magpie Lane. I don't think her landlady would be of much help, do you?'

'Of course, you're right,' Mrs Jeffries replied hastily. She sighed. 'But you know, it might be helpful if you searched Cassie's belongings.'

'Really?'

She gave an embarrassed laugh. 'It's silly of me, sir,

but I couldn't help but think that sometimes women keep little keepsakes of their sweethearts.'

'Do they indeed?' The inspector looked genuinely surprised by this information. 'And what would a keepsake, assuming that she kept something Malcolm had given her, prove?'

'Why, sir, it would prove they'd been together . . .' She broke off and laughed merrily. 'Now, Inspector, you're teasing me. You know very well what I'm getting at.'

Witherspoon smiled uncertainly. He hadn't a clue what his housekeeper was trying to say, but he decided it would probably be a good idea to send Barnes around to search Cassie Yates's belongings. 'Not to worry, Mrs Jeffries,' he said. 'You know how I love my little joke, and come to think of it, you're right. I'll send Barnes around tomorrow to go through the girl's belongings.'

Mrs Jeffries sighed softly. 'Poor girl, how sad that the man she loved ended up being the one who took her life.'

'Yes, tragic,' Witherspoon commented. 'But there is so very much wickedness in this world, it's quite appalling. Why even with all the evidence we've got against this chap, he still insists he didn't do the deed.'

'It's hardly likely that he would confess,' Mrs Jeffries said dryly.

Witherspoon's eyebrows shot up. 'I'm not so sure, Mrs Jeffries. You'd be amazed at how often people do. But Farnsworth isn't one of them. He claims he had a change of heart. He says he spent the rest of the night walking the streets and thinking. Though he has no money, he'd decided that if Cassie was indeed going to bear his child, he'd marry her.'

'And what were they going to live on? Neither of them was employed, nor had they much money.'

Witherspoon shrugged. 'I asked him that. He claimed he was going to sell all his belongings, take the money and Cassie and emigrate to America. Said he wanted to go somewhere where he and Cassie could start again.'

As Witherspoon spoke, Mrs Jeffries could see a rather puzzled expression forming in his eyes. 'What are you thinking, sir?'

'It's quite silly, really,' he admitted with an embarrassed laugh. 'But somehow I almost believed Farnsworth. There was something about him that led me to believe he was telling the truth. Yet he's the only one with the motive and the opportunity. Andrew Lutterbank was home with his family, Emery Clements was visiting his club, and as far as we know, Farnsworth was the only person who knew that Cassie Yates would be at Magpie Lane.'

'What about Antonia Everdene? Or for that matter, the Reverend Everdene? Either of them could have slipped out of the house and followed Cassie.' Mrs Jeffries didn't think this was very likely, but she wanted to make sure they didn't leave any lines of inquiry untouched.

'I don't think so,' the inspector murmured. He suddenly smiled at Mrs Jeffries. 'And it's not because I don't like to believe a woman is as capable of murder as a man. Your stories about some of your late husband's cases have certainly opened my eyes about that particular prejudice.'

Mrs Jeffries was inordinately pleased. Sometimes

she wondered if her dear inspector would ever see the world as it really was rather than as what he wished it to be. 'Then why couldn't either of them have done it?'

'I suppose Miss Everdene could have. She certainly had the motive. She's desperately in love with Farnsworth. But after Farnsworth left, she went into her room and wasn't seen by the servants until the next morning. And she didn't know where Cassie had gone. The reverend couldn't have done the murder – he was indisposed.'

'Oh, I see. He was still drunk.'

'Quite.'

'Will you definitely be arresting Mr Farnsworth tomorrow?'

Witherspoon closed his eyes. 'Yes. The case is circumstantial, but nonetheless it's quite strong.'

Mrs Jeffries didn't sleep well that night. Her mind simply wouldn't stop working. She went over and over every detail of the case and knew that something was wrong, something didn't make sense.

At three in the morning she awoke with two facts pounding in her head. Five hundred pounds . . . She remembered now where she'd heard that figure mentioned before. And Essie Tuttle had told Betsy that she'd seen someone step out of the shadows and follow Cassie Yates on the last night of her life. Malcolm Farnsworth was still with his fiancée then.

Mrs Jeffries threw off her bedclothes, grabbed her robe and hurried out of her room. Almost running, she dashed up the steps to the top floor and tapped on Smythe's door.

'What is it?' Smythe stuck his head out and peered

at her with sleepy eyes. 'Cor, Mrs J, it's the middle of the night.'

'Yes, I know. But there's something I must know. When you went down to the docks, were you able to find out if Sally Comstock got on a ship for Australia?'

He yawned and pushed a lock of hair off his forehead. 'I checked at the Pacific East Line and Merritor's Shipping, they's the two that carries the most passengers from the London docks. They both had sailings on the day Angus Lutterbank was buried, but there weren't no one named Comstock on the passenger manifest.'

'Oh dear,' Mrs Jeffries whispered. For a moment she was terribly afraid. But despite the fear, she knew what she had to do. There was no other way. For she knew who the killer was. If she were wrong, she'd take full responsibility. She could not ask anyone else to do what had to be done. If she were wrong, she would not only be violating man's law, but God's as well.

'What's goin' on, Mrs J?' Smythe gazed at her quizzically.

'Smythe, is there a shovel anywhere about the place?' she asked, ignoring his question.

'There's one in the cooling pantry,' he replied. ''Ere now, what are you up to?'

'Don't ask,' she replied firmly as she turned and started for the stairs. 'It's not the sort of thing I could ever ask anyone else to do. I don't want you involved.'

'Now just a minute 'ere. If'n you think I'm lettin' you toddle off in the middle of the night with a bleedin' shovel all by yerself,' he yelped softly, 'you've got another think comin'.'

She stopped and turned. The coachman was watching

her with a hard, determined expression. 'Smythe,' she said gently, 'I'm going to break the law. I'm going to do something I couldn't in good conscience involve anyone else in. I think I know what happened, but I'm not absolutely certain. However, what I propose to do is the only way I can know for sure. I simply must do it alone. There's too much risk involved—'

'I don't care 'ow much risk there is,' he interrupted. 'I ain't lettin' you go off on your own at this time o' night. You ain't goin' without me,' he said flatly.

'Smythe—'

'No, Mrs J. You jus' give me a minute to get dressed, and don't try leavin' on yer own. Whatever you're up to, I'm goin' with ya.'

She started to argue the point, then realized it was useless. From the fierce expression on his face, she knew Smythe meant to come with her. 'All right, meet me downstairs in five minutes. But I'm warning you, you won't like it one bit.'

Mrs Jeffries was absolutely right. Smythe grimaced as he, Mrs Jeffries and a very jittery Wiggins stopped inside the gate of St Matthew's churchyard.

'Blimey, this is a miserable place,' Wiggins moaned. He gave a quick, terrified glance behind him at the first row of graves. 'Are you sure we ought to be 'ere? It don't seem right.'

'Well no one invited ya to come along,' Smythe snarled.

Wiggins had heard Smythe moving about in his rooms and taken it into his head to go with them, and after a good ten minutes of arguing he had finally convinced Mrs Jeffries and the coachman that he could be of some use. But now, viewing the ghostly churchyard with its eerie tombs and old misshapen headstones, he sincerely wished he'd stayed in bed.

'Which is Angus Lutterbank's grave?' Mrs Jeffries asked briskly. She held the lantern up.

'Over there.' Smythe pointed to the darkest spot in the churchyard. Wiggins groaned.

'Come on, let's get this over with.' Squaring his shoulders and taking a firm grip on the shovel, Smythe headed towards the other side of the graveyard.

Mrs Jeffries held the lantern as the grim trio made their way to Angus Lutterbank's final place of rest. The night was silent. The churchyard, which held generations of London's dead, was so quiet the sound of their footsteps seemed as loud as drumbeats. In the bushes behind the Lutterbank grave, a night scavenger scuttled noisily away from the approaching humans.

'Blimey.' Wiggins jumped and banged into Smythe's broad back. 'What was that?'

'Cor, get off me, ya silly twit. It's just an animal,' Smythe snapped. He put his lantern down, gave Mrs Jeffries a long, level stare and then stuck his shovel deep into the grave. ''Ow deep do you reckon we'll have to go?'

'Not more than a couple of feet,' she murmured, wondering again if she were doing the right thing. But she couldn't think of what else to do, and if she did nothing, Cassie Yates's murderer would get away scot-free. Surely God was more concerned with bringing a killer to justice than a bit of digging about in a spot of hallowed ground. Mrs Jeffries truly hoped so.

For the next twenty minutes the two men dug steadily as Mrs Jeffries held the lamp and watched.

''Ere now,' Smythe mumbled as his shovel dug into something that wasn't soft earth. 'I think we've found what we're lookin' for.' He tossed the shovel onto the small hill of dirt at the side of the shallow pit and dropped to his knees. Using his bare hands, he continued to dig.

A moment later he gasped and straightened. 'You were right, Mrs J. Angus in't the only one buried in this grave.'

'Oh no,' Wiggins moaned. Clenching his teeth and keeping his eyes closed, he dropped to his knees beside the coachman and began to dig too.

They had her uncovered in minutes. Taking a deep breath, Mrs Jeffries stepped closer and held the lantern directly over the body. An ivory-handled knife still protruded from the corpse's ribs. Smythe, his face a mask of horror and revulsion, was breathing raggedly. Wiggins had gone pale. Even Mrs Jeffries felt a shakiness in her knees.

'Who is she?' Wiggins whispered.

Before Mrs Jeffries could answer, Smythe reached down and pulled a bit of tattered cloth from the dead hand. He swallowed and held it close to the lantern.

The cloth had once been a delicate white handkerchief. But in the glow of the light they could see it was badly torn and covered with dark stains. There were embroidered letters in the bottom corner.

'S C,' Smythe said softly. He looked up at Mrs Jeffries, and their gazes met. 'Looks like Sally Comstock never even made it to the docks.'

Their plan was quite simple. As dawn broke, Mrs Jeffries, accompanied by Wiggins, went to Luty Belle's. Smythe kept watch in the churchyard.

Luty listened to them without comment, then ordered Hatchet, who'd been standing in the corner clucking his tongue, over to St Matthew's. The butler didn't look particularly happy about the fact that he was part of their plan. However, he contented himself with a brief speech about grave-robbing, amateur detectives and lunatic Americans before leaving to carry out his part of the scheme.

'Don't pay him no mind,' Luty said as she watched Hatchet's stiff back disappear through the door. 'He's devoted to me. He'll never let on that it was you who dug the girl up.'

'We didn't dig 'er up,' Wiggins protested. 'We didn't even know she were there. It was more like we discovered 'er.'

'Are you absolutely sure about the finger, Luty?' Mrs Jeffries asked anxiously.

'Yes. I'm sure.' Luty grabbed Mrs Jeffries by the arms and ushered her to the front door. 'Now stop yer frettin' and git on home, Hepzibah. None of this is goin' to work if'n the inspector wakes up and finds you gone. You've got to be there when Hatchet shows up with that cockamamie excuse and drags the inspector out to the churchyard. And besides, come this evenin', the killer will be locked up good and tight. I reckon a bit of grave-diggin' is a purty small price to pay for justice.'

CHAPTER ELEVEN

'Now, let me see if I have this right,' Witherspoon said as he stared at Luty Belle Crookshank. 'You sent your butler over to check the date of Angus Lutterbank's death here at St Matthew's, and when he got to the churchyard, he noticed someone had . . . er . . . dug it up? Is that correct?' He glanced from the stern features of Hatchet to Mrs Crookshank.

'Yup, that's right.' Luty grinned. 'Wanted to do some snoopin' on my own afore I told ya what I suspected.'

'And the grave just happened to be open?' The inspector's brows rose. 'That is a remarkable coincidence, wouldn't you say?' He avoided looking down at the exposed body. Starting his day off by examining another corpse was simply too much. He'd delay that unpleasant chore as long as possible.

Hatchet snorted delicately, and Luty Belle threw him a quick glare before she answered the inspector. 'No, I wouldn't say it were a coincidence at all. But if'n you're accusing me of sneakin' over here in the middle of the danged night and diggin' that girl up, you're plum crazy. Take a look at me, Inspector. I'm an old woman, and if'n you think that stiff-necked stuffed shirt of a butler of mine,' she broke off and jabbed her cane in Hatchet's direction, 'would have the stomach for minin' bodies in the middle of the night, you've got another think coming.'

Witherspoon glanced at the impeccably dressed, white-haired servant and sighed. Unfortunately, this eccentric woman was right. He couldn't see either of them doing a spot of grave-digging in the middle of the night. But if they hadn't, then who had? Drat. And he'd thought this miserable case was over and done with. Now he had another body, another murder and the whole horrid business was going to start all over again.

'Besides,' Mrs Crookshank continued earnestly when the inspector remained silent. 'What's it matter who dug the girl up? She's dead, ain't she? Looks to me like it's murder too. There's an ivory-handled dagger sticking outa her ribcage. Now, there's only one person that I know of who'd had a reason to murder the girl, and it sure as shootin' ain't Malcolm Farnsworth, neither.'

'I'm sorry,' Witherspoon said curiously. 'But I don't really see what it is you're getting at. How can you possibly know anything about who took this person's life? We don't even know the identity of the victim.'

'Nells bells, man.' She stamped her cane in frustration. 'Can't you see what's right under yer danged nose? Of course we know who that girl was. Didn't you see them initials embroidered on that hanky? It's Sally Comstock. And the only one who had a reason for wantin' her dead is Andrew Lutterbank. Farnsworth didn't even know the woman. And if'n you don't make tracks, that no-good polecat is gonna get clean outa the country. He and his daddy is fixin' to go to the continent this morning.'

'Gracious, are you certain?' Witherspoon asked in alarm.

'Course I'm certain,' Luty snorted. 'Why do ya think I had Hatchet over here at the crack of dawn checkin' the dates on this tombstone?'

'I beg your pardon?' Witherspoon wished the woman would explain herself a bit more clearly. He was having a most difficult time following her reasoning. 'I'm afraid I don't quite understand.'

'Well, it's simple enough,' she explained. To Luty this part of the plan was the weakest, but as it had been the only idea she and Mrs Jeffries had been able to come up with early this morning, it would have to do. 'Yesterday, when I heard that you was sniffin' around Farnsworth and peggin' him as the killer, I suddenly thoughta something.'

'How on earth did you hear that we were asking Mr Farnsworth to help us with our inquiries?' Witherspoon asked.

'Oh, that don't matter.' Mrs Crookshank waved the question aside and started talking faster. 'Anyhows, I remembered that when they paid Sally Comstock off, they'd supposedly give the girl five hundred pounds. It was the money in the pouch that reminded me o' that. Now, I knew Farnsworth didn't have that kind of cash, so I asked myself how on earth he could have given it to Cassie Yates. Well, he couldn't, could he?'

'Hmmm . . . I'm still not quite sure I follow you,' Witherspoon said hesitantly.

'Then stop interruptin' and listen,' Luty snapped. She'd decided the best defence now was a fast and furious offence. 'Then I recalled that my inquiry agent had told me about a bit of gossip he'd picked up about Cassie Yates. Seems on the day that old Angus was buried, Cassie had snuck out that evenin' and supposedly followed Sally and Andrew down to the docks. Claimed she wanted to say goodbye to her friend.' She laughed cynically. 'Knowin' what I know about that girl, I sure as blazes didn't believe she were sneakin' out to say goodbye. Cassie Yates weren't the kind to git mushy. So I figured that Cassie must have seen somethin' that night she weren't supposed to. I reckon she followed Lutterbank and Sally, saw him kill her with one of those fancy knives of his and then probably sat back and had a good chuckle while Andrew buried the poor girl in Angus's grave.'

'Good gracious, you deduced all that merely from hearing that Cassie Yates had five hundred pounds in her possession?' The inspector gazed at her in awe. Peculiar as the story sounded, it had the ring of truth about it.

'Well.' Luty shrugged modestly. Hatchet sniffed delicately and then turned it into a cough when his employer's eyes narrowed. 'It weren't just that,' she admitted. 'It were the crooked finger too.'

'Crooked finger?' Witherspoon repeated.

'Yup. Braxton Paxton told me that when he went round to Cassie Yates's rooms, the landlady said the man who collected her things the day after she was murdered had a crooked finger.' She shook her head in disgust. 'I don't know why it took so long for me to put it all together. But yesterday, when we come home from talking to you, Mary Sparks said something that reminded me that Andrew Lutterbank's little finger is bent. 'Course, then I knew. The man who collected Cassie's belongin's had to be Andrew, and then it were clear that he was the one that killed her. But it took me a spell to figure out why. At first I figured he musta done her in 'cause he's crazy, well – you've seen his mother. Reckon madness runs purty deep in that family. But I couldn't get that five hundred pounds outa my head. I knew it had somethin' to do with it.'

'Yes,' Witherspoon muttered dazedly. 'I see.'

'Inspector,' a familiar voice called.

'Oh, good.' The inspector turned and saw Constable Barnes and three other uniformed police officers picking their way carefully through the churchyard. 'The lads have arrived. I suppose I'd better take Barnes and perhaps another one and get on over to Mr Lutterbank.'

'You'd best hurry, Inspector,' Luty warned. 'They'll be leavin' the country if you don't git over there and put a stop to it. And once Andrew is out of England, it'll be a cold day in the pits of hell before you can git your hands on him agin.'

'Now, stop that pacin', Hepzibah,' Luty Belle said calmly as she sat in the kitchen of Upper Edmonton Gardens. 'Everythin' went just like we planned. The inspector is probably arrestin' Andrew Lutterbank right now.'

'Are you sure he wasn't suspicious about our story?' Mrs Jeffries asked anxiously.

Luty shrugged. 'He did seem a mite concerned

about that grave being conveniently opened. It's a purty shady story, but I think I convinced him that it didn't matter all that much how the girl got found.'

'And did he understand the significance of the money?'

'Yep, after I explained it, he did.' Luty took a sip of her tea. ''Course gettin' that part in about the crooked finger weren't easy. I ain't sure he really understood what I was tryin' to tell him. But by that time, I had him convinced that if he didn't git over to the Lutterbank house and get his paws on Andrew, the boy was goin' to be gone fer good. The inspector took the dagger with him too. Maybe once Lutterbank sees that the murder weapon can be traced directly to him, he'll git so rattled he'll confess.' Luty suddenly looked around at the empty kitchen. 'Where in tarnation is everybody? I'd think with all the excitement they'd all be here.'

'Mrs Goodge is in the pantry. Wiggins and Smythe are upstairs taking a rest,' Mrs Jeffries replied. 'Remember we did leave poor Smythe to stand guard while I fetched you and Hatchet. Both of them are exhaused. Poor Smythe barely made it in the kitchen door as Hatchet was coming in the front this morning. And oh yes, Betsy's gone over to Putney to get Essie Tuttle. She'll be staying here for a few days while I try and find her another position.' She paused and gave Luty a wide smile. 'Speaking of Miss Tuttle . . .'

Luty raised her hand. 'All right, Hepzibah, you can save your breath. I owe ya. I'll hire the girl. Have Betsy bring her on over to my house this afternoon.'

'Thank you, Luty,' Mrs Jeffries said. Upstairs the front door slammed, and both women jumped.

'Gracious, what was that?' Mrs Jeffries exclaimed as she leapt to her feet. But before she even reached the kitchen steps, a white-faced Inspector Witherspoon stumbled down them and into the kitchen. He threw himself into a chair.

'Inspector, what on earth is the matter?' Mrs Jeffries hurried over to the stove and reached for the kettle. 'You're as pale as a ghost. Let me make you a cup of tea.'

'I'd rather have something a bit stronger, if you don't mind,' Witherspoon croaked. 'I've had a rather unsettling morning. Actually, I'd like a whisky.'

Shocked, Mrs Jeffries whirled around and stared at him. His hair was dishevelled, his lips faintly greenish around the rim, and his hands were shaking.

'Sit still, Inspector,' Luty said as she nimbly leapt to her feet and headed for the stairs. 'I'll git the whisky. Is it in that sideboard in the dining room?'

At Mrs Jeffries's affirmative nod, she disappeared upstairs.

A few moments later she returned, holding the bottle in her arms like a child. 'Hepzibah, you git us some glasses.'

They waited until after the inspector had taken a few good swallows of the liquid before asking any questions.

Finally, when some of the colour had returned to his cheeks, Mrs Jeffries said, 'Now, why don't you tell us what happened?'

Witherspoon took a long, deep breath. 'I suppose I really shouldn't be so upset,' he said slowly. 'I am, after all, a policeman. But honestly, I've never seen anyone shot before my very eyes before.'

'Good gracious,' Mrs Jeffries murmured. 'How utterly dreadful. Oh, you poor man, no wonder you came in here looking as though you'd seen something unspeakable. You had.'

'Who got shot?' Luty asked softly.

The inspector took another quick sip of whisky. 'Andrew Lutterbank. Emery Clements killed him.'

'What!' Mrs Jeffries was stunned. She glanced at Luty and saw the same surprise on her face. 'But why?'

'I suppose I'd better start at the beginning,' Witherspoon said. He was beginning to feel better. But then he'd known he would once he saw his housekeeper and got this horrible experience off his chest. That's why he'd made his excuses and slipped home, telling the Chief Inspector he'd be back directly after lunch.

'I think that's probably wise, sir,' Mrs Jeffries agreed.

'After leaving Mrs Crookshank in the churchyard, I took the dagger and . . .' He paused. 'I assume Mrs Crookshank has told you what happened this morning?'

'Yes, sir.' Mrs Jeffries smiled sympathetically. 'I know all about your adventure. You see, I'd already sent Luty a message that I wanted to see her. I was hoping she'd be able to give Miss Tuttle a position, you see. She very kindly came round and told me about the body in Angus Lutterbank's grave.' She clucked her tongue. 'Really, sir, you've had a terrible day.'

'Yes,' Witherspoon sighed. 'It's been awful. But anyway, let me get on with it. I took the dagger we'd found in Sally Comstock's ribs and, along with Constable Barnes and another officer, went to the Lutterbanks'. It was the most amazing thing, Mrs Jeffries. Remember how I once told you that murderers often confess?'

'I do, indeed, sir.'

'Right, well, Andrew took one look at the dagger and admitted everything.' He flung his arms out in a gesture of disbelief. 'I hadn't even started to ask any questions before he started confessing to two murders. Naturally, I cautioned him that anything he said could be used in a court of law against him but that still didn't shut him up. Andrew wouldn't even listen to his own father. Mr Lutterbank tried to intervene, but he just went on and on. He finally shut up when the butler interrupted him long enough to announce Emery Clements.'

'Is that when Clements shot him?' Luty asked.

Witherspoon shook his head. 'No, that didn't happen till later, till after we'd arrested Lutterbank and taken him into custody. And the irony of it is it was pure chance that Clements happened to come to the Lutterbank home at all. He'd come to give Andrew a bank draft. It seems Clements was the one who'd actually bought Andrew's cottage in Essex.'

'Clements had bought the cottage,' Mrs Jeffries repeated. 'But why?'

'He bought it for Cassie Yates,' the inspector said softly. 'Unfortunately for Andrew Lutterbank, Clements was in the hall long enough to overhear Andrew confessing to murder. I expect the whole household heard the man – he was screaming at the top of his lungs. But right after the butler announced Clements, he suddenly left, and naturally, I thought he was going because, well . . . it's not precisely gentlemanly to hang about and watch a friend get arrested for murder.'

'What happened then, sir?' Mrs Jeffries asked. She

took a small sip from her own glass, grimacing as the whisky burned the back of her throat.

'We arrested Andrew and took him to the police station so he could make a formal statement.' Witherspoon lowered his head and stared at the table. 'While we were taking his statement, the door suddenly flew open and Emery Clements charged in. Before I could do anything, before any of us could make a move, Clements pulled out a revolver and fired twice.' He shuddered and drew a long, deep breath. 'Both shots hit Lutterbank right between the eyes.'

'Lord, sir,' Mrs Jeffries whispered. 'How perfectly awful.'

'It was,' the inspector agreed with feeling. 'Then Clements put the gun down, pushed Andrew out of the chair he'd been sitting in and sat down in his place. That was the worst of it, Clements sitting there talking quite calmly with Lutterbank's corpse at his feet. He confessed to killing Andrew Lutterbank. He said he was avenging Cassie Yates's murder.'

'Good gad almighty,' Luty exclaimed in disbelief. 'You mean that man was stupid enough to walk into a police station and murder someone right under yer nose because of a woman like Cassie Yates? I tell ya, if that don't beat all. The man's ruined his life.'

'Yes, I'm afraid he has,' Witherspoon said. 'But he didn't seem to mind. Said that with her gone his life wasn't worth living anyway. Obviously, he was in love with her. They'd been meeting secretly for months. When he found out for certain that Andrew was responsible for Cassie's murder, he decided to take the law into his own hands.'

'But he defended Farnsworth,' Mrs Jeffries said. 'Clements wouldn't let you search his house yesterday and was going to get a solicitor on his friend's behalf. Why?'

Witherspoon gave her a weary smile. 'I don't think he was defending Malcolm Farnsworth. I think he was planning on killing him. At least, I think he'd have killed him as soon as he knew for sure that Farnsworth was responsible for her murder.'

'You mean he was only pretending to help Malcolm?' Luty asked. 'What makes you think so?'

'Because of the way he spoke about Cassie Yates.' The inspector frowned thoughtfully. 'He was desperately in love with her. He told us he'd arranged to buy Andrew's cottage because he was going to give the place to her as a gift. A lure. He wanted her more than anything in the world.'

'Then why in tarnation didn't he do something about her the past two months?' Luty leaned forward on one elbow. 'Where'd he think the girl was all this time?'

'He said he thought she was abroad.' Witherspoon looked at his almost empty glass of whisky and then shoved it away from him. 'On the day she died, Cassie had led both Clements and Farnsworth to believe she was leaving the country. That's why Farnsworth was so stunned when he found her at the Everdenes'. He fully expected that she was on her way to France.'

'Why did she want everyone to believe she was leaving?' Mrs Jeffries asked. That was one of the few things she hadn't been able to piece together on her own.

'I'm not sure,' the inspector murmured. 'But

Lutterbank told us she'd come to him that morning demanding the five hundred pounds he'd murdered Sally Comstock to keep. Cassie had followed them that night he'd supposedly put Miss Comstock on a ship for Australia, and she'd witnessed the murder. But Cassie bided her time before actually trying to blackmail Lutterbank. She told Andrew and Clements she was going abroad. She'd probably planned to use the money as an added inducement in her campaign to force Malcolm to marry her. Clements told us that when he'd seen Cassie on the morning of the tenth, he'd been the one who told her Farnsworth was going to propose to Antonia Everdene. She wasn't having that. She took the money, forced Miss Sparks to change clothes with her and then confronted Malcolm. Unfortunately, when she left the Everdenes', Andrew followed her. He waited until she was inside the house at Magpie Lane, stabbed her and buried her body in the cellar.' The inspector paused and smiled sadly. 'He committed murder to keep that money and to silence her forever. Imagine how he must have felt when he realized she didn't have it with her. That's why he went to get her things the next day. He wanted to look for the money and make it appear that she'd actually left.' Witherspoon took a deep breath and stood up. 'I'm going back to the station,' he said firmly. 'Much as I'd like to stay here and forget this dreadful day, I've still my duty to perform.'

It was very late that evening before Mrs Jeffries and the others could gather round the kitchen table.

''Ere I was hanging on to that silly Essie Tuttle

and helpin' her pack with that awful Miss Everdene screechin' at both of us, and all the time, the case were comin' to a close.' Betsy scowled heavily. 'It don't seem right. I missed everythin'.'

'I don't think you really missed all that much, Betsy,' Mrs Jeffries said kindly. 'Watching one man shoot another certainly isn't a very nice sight.'

'I still don't understand.' Wiggins yawned. ''Ow did you know that Sally Comstock would be buried in Angus's grave?'

'She's already explained that twice,' Mrs Goodge complained. 'Haven't you been listenin'?'

'That's quite all right, Mrs Goodge. It's no wonder Wiggins can't concentrate. He didn't get much sleep last night.' Mrs Jeffries smiled at her two fellow conspirators. 'I suspected Sally was in the grave because of the amount of money that was found in the pouch Cassie gave Mary Sparks for safe-keeping. If you'll recall, the first time Luty Belle came to ask for our help, she made a very casual comment to the effect that Andrew Lutterbank's indiscretions had cost him five hundred pounds and a trip to Australia. When Smythe confirmed that there was no record of Sally ever having been a passenger to Australia, I decided that Andrew had probably killed her and buried her body in a convenient place. In this case, Angus's grave. The earth was still nice and soft; it wouldn't have been very difficult for a healthy young man to reopen it and put her inside.'

'You were takin' a chance there, Mrs J,' Smythe said. 'I only checked with two lines that goes to Australia. What if she'd left from another port?'

'I was hoping the Lutterbanks were in such a hurry to get rid of the girl, they booked her passage on a vessel leaving that very day,' Mrs Jeffries answered.

''Ow come a rich man like 'im did 'er in for a piddlin' little amount like five hundred quid?' Wiggins asked.

'Five hundred pounds is a lot of money,' Mrs Goodge said. 'Eat some more of them cakes, boy. You've missed too many meals lately.' She shoved the plate closer to the footman.

'It wasn't just the money,' Mrs Jeffries said softly. 'I think that perhaps Luty was right. There is madness in that family. Andrew was tainted with it. I think he enjoyed killing those women.'

'Well,' Betsy said, 'I still don't quite see 'ow you knew it were 'im that did the killin'. Were it just the money that gave you the hint?'

'No, it was also the fact that you reported that Essie Tuttle had said that when Cassie left the Everdene house, a man stepped out of the shadows and followed her.' Mrs Jeffries explained. 'I knew that man couldn't have been Malcolm Farnsworth. Essie said he was still in the house when she went back inside. So I decided that the murderer was most likely the man who'd followed Cassie, and not Malcolm. For one thing, if Farnsworth had murdered her, he wouldn't have buried her body in the cellar. He knew that Magpie Lane wasn't going to be widened for a road. Why would he have buried the girl when he knew perfectly well the property along there was going to be dug up for an underground railway? Clements knew the same thing. So I suspected that neither of them were the killers. That left Andrew Lutterbank.'

'But he was supposed to have been at home that night,' Mrs Goodge put in.

'That's another reason I suspected him.' She smiled wryly. 'How many of us know exactly where we were on any particular night several months ago? Yet when the inspector asked where he'd been, his father immediately stated he was at home. I knew that was a lie.'

'You think his father might have suspected Andrew of bein' the killer?' Smythe asked as he poured himself another cup of tea.

'I'm certain of it.' Mrs Jeffries yawned. 'I think he knew all too well what kind of evil his son was capable of doing. That's probably why he suddenly decided to take young Andrew on a business trip. He wanted him out of the country, out of the reach of Scotland Yard.'

Betsy sighed. 'Well, it's over now, at least for us.'

'Too bad it ain't over for the inspector,' Smythe said. 'Looks like there's goin' to be a bit of a ruckus on this one.' He scowled and lifted his chin to meet Mrs Jeffries's eyes. 'You think 'e'll be all right?'

'He'll be just fine,' she announced. 'As soon as this case is officially closed, he's going off to the country for a few days to visit friends. It'll do him the world of good.'

Betsy suddenly giggled. 'Speakin' of the country, you should 'ave seen Hatchet's face when I took Essie to Luty Belle's. 'E didn't spend two minutes with her before he looked like 'e'd like to put her on a train and send 'er to parts unknown.'

They all laughed.

'Speaking of Luty,' Mrs Jeffries said when the merriment had died down, 'she sent me a note this afternoon.

When the inspector leaves for the country, she wants to take us all on a nice outing.'

'Maybe she'll take us to one of them posh restaurants over on the Strand,' Betsy said excitedly.

'I could fancy a day at the races meself,' Smythe muttered.

'Nah, let's hope she takes us to the circus,' Wiggins countered.

'An outing on the river would be nice,' Mrs Goodge said thoughtfully.

'I was rather hoping for a concert or perhaps the ballet,' Mrs Jeffries interjected. 'Mozart would be very nice.'

EPILOGUE

S HE TOOK THEM to a music hall. Mrs Jeffries felt
she really ought to protest, but when she saw how
excited the others were, she simply didn't have the
heart. And she was rather curious herself. She'd never
been to a music hall.

Dressed in their best and accompanied by Luty and
Hatchet, they drove off in high spirits.

The place was warm, garish and hazed with smoke
from dozens of cigars. The noise level was so loud, Mrs
Jeffries couldn't hear herself think.

Luty tapped her cane in time to the tinny music from
the piano, Smythe and Wiggins almost got cricks in
their necks from stretching to get a better view of the
can-can dancers, and Betsy and Mrs Goodge laughed
themselves silly at the bawdy jokes from the vaudeville
comic.

All in all, everyone had a wonderful time. Even
Hatchet unbent far enough to join in the raucous
singalong.

The evening ended far too quickly. As Luty's coach
drew up outside the front door of Upper Edmonton

Gardens, Mrs Jeffries leaned forward and said, 'How's Essie Tuttle getting along, Luty?'

Luty cackled with laughter. 'Oh, she's gettin' along just fine. It's Hatchet I'm worried about. The girl's givin' 'im fits. Silly old fool took it into his head to teach her to read. Now he's complainin' that that's all she wants to do.'

Betsy giggled. 'Honestly, men. They think they own you just because they gives you a little 'elp now and again.'

Smythe snorted. 'Yeah, and you females spend all yer time runnin' a poor man ragged.'

'What's that supposed to mean?' Betsy demanded indignantly.

'You know very well what it means.' The coachman glared at her. 'You was runnin' that poor lad ragged tonight. He musta fetched you three glasses of lemonade.'

''E offered,' she sniffed, 'and besides, I didn't invite 'im to sit next to me.'

'You didn't discourage 'im, neither,' Smythe snapped. 'And I don't think it's right you agreein' to see 'im again.'

'I didn't agree to see him again,' Betsy defended herself. 'He just asked me if I were interested in spiritualism, and I said I was. It's an interestin' subject.'

'Spiritualism,' Mrs Jeffries exclaimed. 'Good gracious, you're not thinking of going to visit a spiritualist with this young man, are you?'

'I'd like ta go too,' Luty put in. 'I've always wanted to go to one of them there séances. Used to be a fortune-teller in San Francisco I'd go see. She were right good too.'

Mrs Jeffries and Smythe both scowled at Luty, who ignored them.

Betsy tossed her blonde curls and frowned at the coachman. 'Oh, I don't see why you're gettin' so miserable all of a sudden. I'm not goin' to see Edmund again.'

'Good,' Smythe mumbled. He reached for the door latch. 'I don't want you gettin' into trouble.'

'Don't be silly,' Betsy replied airily as she stepped out of the coach behind Luty and Mrs Jeffries. 'What kind of trouble could I possibly get into by going to a séance?'